THEN . . .

In the year 1585, Queen Elizabeth commanded Lord Humphrey to marry Lady Caroline. It was the only way to infiltrate Castle Tregenna, suspected base of Catholic conspirators sworn to kill the Queen. But Lady Caroline proved to be more woman than Lord Hap, as he preferred to be called, had bargained for. She aroused a passion that blinded him to treachery and danger.

AND NOW . . .

En route to Castle Tregenna to bid on a set of Medici chess pieces, antiques dealer Caroline DeVries plunges over a cliff in her car. Her spirit is summoned from the wreck by Lord Hap, the Castle's resident ghost. She does not know it yet, but they have met and loved long ago. Once again, they face intrigue within the Castle walls. Once again, the promise of their love seems impossible to fulfill.

Lord
Hap
BY MARILYN K. DICKERSON

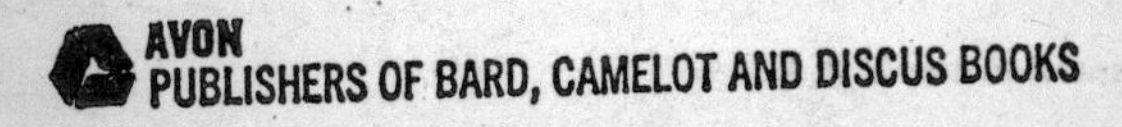
AVON
PUBLISHERS OF BARD, CAMELOT AND DISCUS BOOKS

This is a work of fiction. The characters and events described are purely products of the author's imagination and bear no relationship to real persons or events, past or present.

LORD HAP is an original publication of Avon Books. This work has never before appeared in book form.

AVON BOOKS
A division of
The Hearst Corporation
959 Eighth Avenue
New York, New York 10019

Published by arrangement with the author
Library of Congress Catalog Card Number: 80-65413
ISBN: 0-380-75572-6

First Avon Printing, June, 1980

AVON TRADEMARK REG. U.S. PAT. OFF. AND IN OTHER COUNTRIES, MARCA REGISTRADA, HECHO EN U.S.A.

Printed in the U.S.A.

To Bill Dickerson, friend and husband; Myrtle Archer, friend and teacher; and Writers West, friends and critics.

Chapter 1

CAROLINE

When I, Caroline deVries, first set foot in Castle Tregenna, the prospect of becoming its resident ghost was the last thought in my mind. Especially since the castle, a formidable heap of Cornish rock and legend, was already inhabited by a historical spook by the name of Lord Humphrey Algernon Pettigrew, or Lord Hap, as he introduced himself. Not that I wouldn't have been pleased to death, if you'll pardon the expression, to reside in such a splendid example of fifteenth-century architecture. Impressive too, were its contents: rooms of exquisitely carved furniture, massive armoires and sideboards, priceless collections of silver and ivory. Indeed, for me, a Knightsbridge antique dealer, to die and go to Tregenna was the equivalent of heavenly attainment. Or at least it might have been had my demise occurred under less mysterious circumstances. One reads of the victims of foul play whose restless souls are unable to find peace until properly avenged. Perfectly willing to humor the idea, I found myself stymied to know how to pursue it or where to begin. Someone had obviously contrived to end my life, and with apparent success. But why?

My story began three months ago as I hurriedly unlocked the front door of my shop to answer a frantically jangling telephone.

"Good morning, Miss deVries. This is Peter Ormsby."

The phone nearly slid out of my fingers. The Lord of Tregenna, calling me? I had met Sir Peter only once before. On that occasion I'd audaciously approached him with an offer to buy his renowned set of carved chessmen, reputedly once owned by Catherine de Medici. As I recalled, his response had been less than civil. Now he was approaching me? I answered in my coolest professional voice. "Why, this is a surprise, Sir Peter. In what way may I serve you?"

"How lovely to hear your voice again, my dear," he purred.

I stared in astonishment at the telephone receiver. This was not the Sir Peter I remembered. Despite my suspicions I felt compelled to at least listen. Tregenna represented a vast storehouse of priceless antiquities and I'd have given my right arm to acquire even a small consignment to sell through my shop. Normally when Sir Peter bought or sold, he dealt through Sotheby's in London.

Sir Peter slid over my prolonged silence. "The reason that I've called, Miss deVries, is to invite you to Tregenna. Would you be able to come this afternoon? I'd appreciate your appraisal of the Medici set and I would like to invite you to make a bid on it as well. I realize this is rather short notice . . . Hello? Hello, Miss deVries? Have we been cut off?"

I heard the hollow clack-clack as he depressed the telephone rest, and the impatient rush of his breath into the mouthpiece. Sir Peter, I remembered, possessed the rather irritating habit of stroking his right eyebrow as he spoke, and if perturbed, was inclined to pluck at the hairs themselves. I pictured him making that very gesture now.

"Uh, yes, of course I'm still here, Sir Peter . . ." I hedged, still trying to discern the hook I suspected lurked in such tempting bait. "I—I have an appointment this afternoon but I'm certain I can reschedule it."

His sticky charm again oozed over the line. "Ah, I thought I could count on you, my dear, and of course I'm relying on your absolute discretion as well. I do have your promise that this matter will be kept solely between the two of us . . . ?" He didn't allow me to answer. "Yes, of course I do. For one so young and, may I say, lovely, you have a remarkable reputation as a collector, Miss . . . may I call you Caroline?"

I grimaced at Sir Peter's pretense of familiarity. In our brief encounter he had impressed me as a rigidly aloof nobleman, highly jealous of his station. What was his game now? "Why, of course, *Peter,*" I answered sweetly and could almost see him draw back, affronted.

"Uh, yes, of course." He cleared his throat. "Well, then, until later, Miss . . . *Caroline.*" Again, not waiting for a response, he rang off, his cultured words in their clipped, enunciated tones, still ringing in my head. I sat distracted for a long moment, gnawing at my lower lip. A voice in the back room of my brain was saying: don't go. . . . Abruptly I stood up, almost knocking over the Queen Anne chair in which I was sitting. "Oh, shut up," I snapped at myself. In my business I couldn't afford offending Sir Peter, whatever my suspicions.

Promptly I phoned Aunt Cleo, set the Closed sign in the front window, and drove home to the flat we shared on Bartholomew Street. Cleo wasn't really a relative, but fourteen years ago she had taken me in after my parents had drowned in a sailing accident. She and my mother had been girlhood friends.

When Cleo's father died of a stroke, she ably stepped in and continued the family antique business. As a result, I grew up surrounded by the whimsical fantasy world of other ages, growing to love the material remnants of the past. Curled in a looming wing chair at the rear of the shop, I'd sit raptly for hours devouring the contents of Cleo's vast reference library. While other children immersed themselves in fairy tales, I traveled the wondrous, imagined paths of history. I could sit and stare at a French wedding clock or an exquisitely figured Wedgewood bowl and conjure the fictitious faces and emotions of those who'd possessed them. It was a marvelous game, and my imagined worlds often became more real to me than the busy, trafficked London streets just beyond our door. Upon completing my education I naturally joined Aunt Cleo in the business of collecting and selling antiques.

Now, at the age of twenty-six, I regard myself well settled in the profession. Only yesterday, Benson Higby, a recognized authority among collectors and a friendly rival, had grudgingly acknowledged my expertise. I'd outmaneuvered him in the purchase of a buhl desk, and he, in his dry, humorless fashion, had complained. "There ought to be a law against you, Caroline deVries. You beguile a man with the face and figure of a Botticelli Venus and then you confound the poor bastard with shrewd business acumen—bah!" He dismissed me with a deprecating wave of his hand and rudely walked off.

But I had long ago learned that Benson Higby never stooped to insult an inferior. Secretly flattered, I laughed, calling after the portly figure in his unpressed gray suit, "From you, Benson, I consider that practically an endorsement."

Turning right onto Bartholomew Street I spied a parking spot directly in front of 611. I eased the Escort into the space with a few deft turns of the wheel and hurried up the steps. Aunt Cleo met me at the door, her brown eyes gleaming over the half-crescent reading glasses perched on the end of her nose. As usual, her gray hair was flawlessly dressed, drawn to the top of her head and fashioned in perfect, sculptured curls. She wore the black and green caftan I'd given her for Christmas. "Bravo, my dear," she hailed with a smile. "If you can wrap up the purchase of this Medici set from Lord Peter . . ."—Cleo spread her hands in an all-encompassing gesture—"the sky's the limit."

I agve her a quick hug, not willing to worry her with my vague suspicions, and walked quickly into the bedroom. "I'm sorry to rush off like this, Cleo," I called over my shoulder. "But I must get on the road post haste. It's stopped raining for the moment but it's still threatening, and I don't cherish the idea of driving all the way to Tregenna in bad weather. Oh, by the way . . ." I paused in the doorway. "Be a darling and feed Siegfried for me, will you? And be sure to remember his vitamins and his—"

Cleo threw up her manicured hands, jangling her gold bracelets. "Oh, for heaven's sake, Caroline, you treat that silly parakeet like an idiot child." Her sternly pursed lips split in a helpless grin. "Yes, of course you know that I will, dear. Don't worry about a thing but putting over this deal."

Ten minutes was all I needed to toss a nightie, robe, slippers, blouse and cosmetics into a travel bag. Cleo gave me a quick kiss on the cheek and then held me away slightly, her hands on my shoulders. The shrewd eyes behind the ridiculous glasses narrowed. "Are you certain everything's all right, Caroline? If there's something troubling you about this trip, perhaps I should go along with you."

I faked a cheerful grin. "I'm a big girl, Auntie, and this is my big chance to make good. So bug off, will you, darling?"

I last glimpsed her concerned face through the glass panel in the front door. She waved a reluctant goodby as I pulled on my sheepskin coat and bolted for the jaunty little Ford Escort still warm at the curb. Mastering my concentration, I weaved through London toward M-3 and my journey south.

So determined was I to reach my destination, I was scarcely conscious of the towns I passed through. Normally on buying jaunts I set a leisurely pace, visiting the thatched and beamed antique shops along the way. But this time my urgency sent me flying blindly to Tregenna.

M-3 ended abruptly near Basingstoke and the highway narrowed to a two-lane thoroughfare to Salisbury. Darkening hedgerows loomed like tall sentinels along the road, and ancient elms, in the crowding dusk, lifted entwined branches high overhead. The little yellow car hurtled through the tunnel of greenery. My hands guided the wheel, but another force beyond my comprehension insidiously charted the course.

The storm I'd hoped to leave behind in London followed hard on my heels. Black and rain-laden clouds rumbled in pursuit. As I cleared the outskirts of Salisbury, three silver-white bursts of lightning exploded across the crouching field to my right, their knifing strokes slashing open the skies as a barrage of water plummeted earthward. The car shuddered under the violent onslaught of rain and wind, but continued on its way. I sighed with relief and switched on the headlights and windshield wipers, anxiously leaning forward, trying to penetrate the wall of water. The mundane whish-thump of the windshield wipers was comforting but their futile efforts were no match against the punishing deluge of the storm. It was twilight now and I could barely make out the narrow ribbon of the road directly ahead. I shivered in my sheepskin coat, aware of the cold creeping into my bones. It still wasn't too late to turn back to Salisbury. Mrs. Dundee, who operated a small pension there, could surely find accommodations for me. Often I stayed with her when buying trips proved too attractive to return to London. And . . . but my hands froze on the wheel. What was wrong with me, anyway? A little rain wasn't going to stop me now that I had come this far. I drew in a deep breath to ease the tension that felt like a weight pressing against my rib cage. And with a defiance that surprised me, my foot bore down on the accelerator.

For the next three hours, the storm dogged my progress like an avenging angel until at last I turned in between the massive stone pedestals that marked the entrance to Tregenna Castle. No light welcomed me but I had expected none. The central building was situated on the furthermost quarter of the property, facing the sea. From the main road a narrow track, reduced now to a muddy trail, idled through the sodden, night-cloaked parks and forest of Tregenna.

I remembered that nearing the castle the road clung desperately to the cliff's edge that fell precipitously away to the sea below. On a bright, sun-filled day the rampaging surf had terrified me. I shut my mind to the fear binding my chest. Abruptly I jammed on the brakes. The car jerked to a stop and I stared incredulously at the yellow detour sign lopsidedly set at the forked juncture of the path. A detour sign? Out here in the middle of nowhere? I shut my tired eyes for a moment, but when I opened them again the sign, a watery blur caught in the yellow beams of the headlights, was still there. I was too tired to argue. I knew Sir Peter to be eccentric at times, but this verged on the ridiculous. I set the car briefly in reverse and turned up the designated road.

A few minutes later the lights of Tregenna appeared like glowing embers through the storming blackness. I had just eased my weary lungs in a long, grateful sigh when the front end of the Escort dropped sickeningly forward, taking my heart with it. The revving engine ground fiercely like a wounded animal. Only when my eyes focused on the bursting waves illuminated in the pendulum swing of the headlights did I realize the front wheels hung in empty space, the car teetering on the edge of the cliff. A woman's shrill, terrified scream rang out again and again, deafening my senses. The car lurched forward, balanced, and then arched slowly and gracefully toward the waiting rocks below.

Chapter 2

Everyone at some time considers the prospect of dying. I hadn't imagined my death would be so precipitate. One moment my own agonized screams seared across my brain, the rocky shore rushing up to meet me and then—then. A vacuum of silence embraced me. Time crouched, an entity abandoned and dismissed. Never had I known such a sense of unfettered peace as I floated upon the tide of infinity. Gently soaring, weightless, the myriad cells of my being intermingled with the infinite energy of all creation. Oddly, I was unafraid. I drifted and dreamed and knew not but that I would open my eyes and find myself safely tucked in my own bed on Bartholomew Street. But whether such a reality would materialize seemed of little significance.

I do not know how long I remained in that euphoric corridor. But gradually, even reluctantly, in a swirl of vapors, I emerged to find myself desposited on the mossy green rocks where the yellow Escort lay mangled in a smoking ruin. On the driver's side, the window sparkled in a mosaic of shattered glass. Through the broken window I saw the motionless body slumped sideways, buckled into the seat. My head was flung back, cradled in the nest of my own dark hair. From between pale, parted lips, blood angled a crimson track across chin and throat to form a puddle in an inching smear that spread over my breasts. Viewing my broken body I was filled with glutted, suffocating sadness. I could not cry, but the silvered rain slanting with the wind made my tears. Umbrageous waves, dark cylinders of rage, flung themselves upon the rocks, spewing the diffused thunder of my despair.

Suddenly the storm quieted, although the thrashing animation continued its weird, silent dance around me.

Hovering by my side, a gentle voice, tinged with its own sadness said: "Bear up, Mistress, and be of good cheer. Often being dead ain't half so bothersome as being alive. But then, I've been dead for four hundred years and confounded in my mortal coil for only thirty-one."

Unaccustomed to the weightlessness, I swung in a clumsy, slow-motion half turn. I thought that were I still capable of it, I might faint. "Who—who are you?" I managed to choke out.

Comprised of only a suspended head, the apparition beamed beatifically, baring a crescent of white teeth that glowed in the darkness. He bowed his sleek black head formally and a detached hand, long-fingered and sensitive, stroked a brief, pointed beard. "Lord Humphrey Algernon Pettigrew, Mistress, at your service," he said. "But to my friends I answer to Lord Hap."

I looked up at him out of the corner of my eye. If the position of his head was any indication, he was quite tall and, somehow I fancied, broad of shoulder, too. My mouth kept opening to speak and closing again on dry silence. Words caught and died in my throat before they could be uttered. How odd, I thought. My corporal remains were slumped in the crushed wreckage a few feet away. Why was I *still* experiencing such forceful physical sensations? And to such a degree that my throat could constrict in fear and the echo of a dead heart still so energetically thump in my chest?

I caught Lord Hap's bright gaze studying the inner turmoil that must have been reflected on my face. His smile was sympathetic. "You've only just been severed from life," he said kindly. "It takes a while to adjust, you know. Liken it to an amputated foot that continues to itch long after its separation from the leg. Only moments ago you parted from your physical self and its entourage of emotions. It's perfectly natural that their residual essence lingers."

His explanation seemed so logical I wondered why I hadn't thought of it myself. A sense of gratitude welled up inside of me toward this kindred spirit. "Thank you, m'lord. I can't tell you what a comfort it is to have someone, well, introduce me to uh—to uh . . . Just where is it that we are?" I gave a quick glance around. "I mean, I know that this is Tregenna, but in the *metaphysical* scheme of things, *where* are we?"

In a concerted effort to answer my question, his dark brows drew together. Lord Hap now materialized down to the waist and then revealed fine muscular legs clad to the knee in soft Italian leather. Sartorially splendid, he wore a closely fitted red velvet doublet. The stiff ruff about his neck gleamed white against the blackness of the crisp, pointed beard, and the glint in his eye seemed strangely familiar. He was, however, reluctant to give me a direct answer.

"Ah, Mistress," he purred happily. "T'is so good to have another soul to whom I may address myself—I—" A flap of wings interrupted him and angrily Lord Hap jerked his head around to stare loathfully at a ghostly parrot that swooped in from the ether to land on his shoulder. In a noisy commotion of threshing feathers the bird missed his footing, overbalanced first forward and then backwards, and had the gentleman not lifted a steadying hand for his assistance, no doubt would have fallen. Weaving drunkenly on his perch, the parrot cocked his balding green head and leered at me with one yellow eye. The most salacious laugh I'd ever heard rattled out of the open beak. "Ah, yer a foine strappin' wench, ya are . . ." he caroled in a disturbingly human voice. "Whatever yer price—to bed! To bed, wench . . ."

Lord Hap gritted his teeth as though in pain. He was apparently as embarrassed as I was startled. Carefully he picked a stray feather from his coat and, holding it with obvious distaste between thumb and forefinger, flicked it to oblivion. *"Beastly* creature," he muttered, "been moulting all over me for four hundred years." Ignoring us, the bird settled himself on Lord Hap's shoulder and, closing his one good eye, lapsed into an inebriated stupor.

"Ah, *ha,* and what is your pet's name, m'lord?" I asked, attempting to overcome the awkward silence.

Still quietly livid, Lord Hap hunched his red-clad shoulders. "If you must know, Mistress, that foul bird answers to the name of Perrigrine." The white ruff circling the lord's neck bobbed up and down as he swallowed in agitation. "He—*we* shared a common tomb and alas, shared a common destiny ever since that ill-fated day. A dozen lifetimes of hell on earth with none of the baser pleasures to sweeten its passing." With a faint moan, my Lord Hap withdrew into a dark reverie.

I reached out to pat his arm before I realized he could not know the comfort of my touch. My hand merely passed through his sleeve like two shadows merging. Our minds had blended, but a simple expression of compassion was barred to us. He'd said that he and the parrot shared a common destiny. Perhaps entering the ghostly state together allowed them a camaraderie, if even a hostile one, that was denied to me. Sadly my heart sank into a chasm of emptiness. For the first time I became fully aware of the hopelessness of my situation. Neither heaven nor hell lay claim to me, and better even the latter than this limbo of nothingness.

Perrigrine muttered loudly in his sleep, calling, "Another tankard of ale, wench," and again fell silent.

The bird's outburst must have reached Lord Hap in his brooding reverie for he turned to me, a slight apologetic smile lifting the corners of the sensitive mouth. Without speaking, my desperation was communicated through my thoughts.

"Aye, Mistress," he acknowledged quietly. "I read your panic and recognize it as my own all these lonely years. Believe me, if it were within my power to set you free, I would do so even though your brief presence has already brightened this dreary existence for me."

I met the deep longing in his eyes and shuddered, moved by a forgotten memory of another time.

Lord Hap looked away, tugging at his beard. He sighed heavily as though resolving some predicament with which he struggled. "Mistress—" he began slowly.

I interrupted. "Please, m'lord, my name is Caroline deVries. *Please* call me Caroline."

Now he laid his regard upon me, light shining in his large brown eyes. "Ah, yes, Caroline," he murmured, savoring the word upon his tongue. "Caroline—sweet music to the heart, yet womanly to the eye and strong. How well it suits you, Lady Caroline."

His voice caressed my soul and set my cheeks, I was certain, glowing in the wintry darkness. I decided immediately that I could better cope with his depression than with his unpredictable ardor. Energetically I launched into another subject. "M'lord, I really think we should put our heads together and—and establish some plan of action for getting ourselves out of . . . whatever predicament . . . we're, uh, in . . ." I finished weakly.

An amused grin spread across his face. Why did I feel that he knew exactly what I meant, no matter what I said?

He tapped the tips of his fingers together, his eyes two dancing demons. His tone remained perfectly sober. I suspected he was humoring me. "Ah, yes, you're quite right, Mistr—uh, Caroline. Now, let me see. . . . Obviously we've *both* been victimized by a dark deed that prevents our souls the solace of final rest. And until we apprehend the perpetrator we are forever doomed to—" Lord Hap's levity faded as his brows shot up. "Is that true, Caroline? Were you the victim of foul play?"

Briefly I related the events that brought me to Tregenna, touching on Lord Ormsby's sudden offer, the Medici set and the detour sign responsible for sending me hurtling to an untimely end.

He listened patiently and when I finished, nodded slowly, tugging on the point of his short beard. "Well, that explains graphically your presence here," he agreed. "As no doubt you've already concluded, I, too, am a dupe of circumstances; hence this prolonged haunting." He tilted his head to one side, contemplating my face. His level gaze made me blink away my stare. "But ya know, Caroline, I have the strangest feeling that you are the catalyst that's going to work a miracle for me. Because oddly enough, my lady, 'twas a Lord Ormsby four hundred years ago that featured prominently in my own ignominious demise. Rather a coincidence, wouldn't you say, my pretty lady, with your golden hair and eyes the hue of Spanish sherry?"

I stared blankly at Lord Hap, struck with horror that not only was he a ghost but perhaps a mad one at that. Hair of gold? Eyes like Spanish sherry? My hair was russet brown and my eyes green. Fear curled inside me but I wrestled it away. I'd find no answers in this storm-washed landscape.

I struggled to regain some semblance of calm, and

faced Lord Hap with what felt like a frozen smile. "I think it's time we were on our way to Tregenna, m'lord," I suggested. It seems to be the focal point in our respective tragedies. "Perhaps you'll show me the way?" I faked an I'll-follow-you-to-the-ends-of-the-earth expression and advanced toward him expectantly.

Lord Hap caught and held my gaze for a long, compelling moment, I suspected weighing and measuring my intentions and then capitulating, a faint whimsical smile drew up the corners of his mouth. "Yes, of course, Lady Caroline," he vouchsafed smoothly. He inclined his dark head toward a patch of tall trees thrashing wildly in the clutch of the winds. "Follow me, sweet Caroline, and I'll introduce you to a pack of villains you'll not soon forget." He paused again. About to continue, he checked himself instead. An almost crafty look of speculation flickered across his face. Without further comment he ruthlessly jostled the sleeping bird on his shoulder and the three of us swept unhampered through the howling night toward the castle walls of Tregenna.

Chapter 3

Writhing sycamores parted before our gliding advance. Across an expanse of deer park alive with cavorting shadows, the rigid silhouette of Tregenna reared jagged-toothed turrets against the animated sky. As we neared, the throaty roar of the stormy Atlantic grew louder, for Tregenna clung to a lofty crest of granite with its back to the sea. The rear of the great house sheared abruptly to the pounding waves below. The sea's gnawing rasp filled the air. Unseen, it imparted to the looming structure the essence of a menacing creature ready to pounce and devour.

Glowing mullioned windows on the second level emanated a subdued evidence of occupancy but issued no welcome. In the same sense, if one approached hell and found it appropriately lighted, there would be little comfort in knowing the devil was at home. I paused, reluctant to continue. Fear and awe of the massive walls crowned with castellated towers held me back, while another emotion, elusive and undefined, prodded me forward. Lord Hap, choosing to ignore my cowardly hesitancy, surged on. His name a faint plea on my lips, I bolted after him.

An arched door built of aged beams gave access to the inner court. Lodged in the gray slate above the entry, an iron lantern swayed to the wind's mad fancy, metal joints shrieking a cacophony of warning to all who dared enter. Its light created a crazy midnight dance of shadows that found no partner in me. I realized that my spectral image could not mingle with its cast radiance and for a moment I was overcome with sadness at the loss of my shadow.

Looking up, I was embarrassed by Lord Hap's witness to my private struggles, but he chose not to take issue with me. He merely nodded casually toward the portal. "Come, Caroline," he urged quietly, and stepped through the thick wooden paneling. I stared at his broad back disappearing through the solid framework and found myself alone outside the entrance gate. A stab of panic gagged me and I could only whisper his name. "Lord Hap! Lord Hap . . . Where are you? . . ."

I heard a low, amused chuckle. Then a red-clad arm, pristine white ruffles at the wrist, appeared through the door and beckoned me. "Come along, Lady Caroline," a laughing voice called. "You'll not find the passing difficult. Remember you've no physical body to restrain your progress. Just step through, Caroline. You can do it, lass, you can do it."

His mocking tone reminded me of my childhood vacations to Lake Falmouth and my cousin Tony's childish taunts, attempting to lure me into icy waters. "Come on, Caro, you big sissy, stick your big toe in the water. It won't kill ya. Stick your big toe . . ."

This time Lord Hap had not chosen to humor me. His marvelously deep-throated laugh sounded again and my reluctance slipped away. Holding out a tentative hand before me, I bounded through the closed gate as though it did not exist, abandoning as I did the relative idea that it was *I* who no longer existed.

We did not linger in the courtyard but passed immediately into the huge central hall. The temperature was hardly warmer than outside. Bare stone walls rose to a high, vaulted ceiling from which hung a large circular chandelier of crude iron. Four indifferent candles emitted a sallow light, barely capable of illuminating the distant corners. I jumped like a thief as a hidden door was flung open and banged against the wall. A stooped old man trudged across the long chamber, muttering to himself and bearing an oversized tray, his breath condensing in icy puffs behind him. I agilely stepped out of his way to avoid what I still imagined would be a collision.

At polished double doors he hoisted the tray to one shoulder, knocked and gained entrance. I glimpsed a brightly lighted room of considerable elegance behind the door, vaguely recalling it to be one of three reception chambers located on the second level. The heated argument that had been going on inside ceased with the old servant's appearance. Waving to Lord Hap to follow, I slipped into the room before the door slid shut. I still preferred the customary manner of passing from place to place. Lord Hap materialized immediately beside me with an irritating smirk on his face.

My annoyance dissolved in the dazzle of an antique collector's dream. The contents of the room met in a collision of styles and periods, the priceless treasures amassed through the centuries by the Lords of Tregenna. Seventeenth-century Brussels tapestries, in Rubens style, warmed the high stone walls. Buhl desks and tables inlaid with pewter and tortoiseshell stood beside Empire chairs and baroque settees. Lighted cabinets displayed elaborate arrangements of bejeweled trinkets sparkling in precious splendor. A priceless collection of clocks in dorée, porcelain and enamel measured out the minutes with precise, staccato strokes.

"You sigh with the contentment of a sow wallowing in her pen, dear Caroline," Lord Hap observed dryly.

I shrugged him off with a toss of my head. But I couldn't take my eyes from a brilliant collection of early Murano glass ablaze in a standing display case. A faint breeze tickled my ear and I turned my head abruptly.

Lord Hap stood next to me, his lips puckered, his face filled with mischief.

"Well, really, Lord Hap," I admonished. "*You* may not have an appreciation for the finer things in life but I—"

"Nay, Mistress," he rejoined with sudden anger. "It's not that I lack for appreciation but rather that prolonged proximity breeds contempt. No man loves his jail, Caroline. You forget that I've inhabited these walls for four centuries." His voice dropped and he grinned evilly. "Surely you may appreciate that some of their charm wears thin." Impatience flashed in the dark eyes. "So shall we get on with the business at hand—namely, how the flaming fires of hell we're to escape this servitude of the dead and nearly damned?"

Lord Hap's outburst shook me. My remark had been callous and insensitive. I nodded, properly chastened. "Yes, of course, my lord," I mumbled. "If you'll be so good, please introduce me to our companions."

Three people in various moods were positioned around the room. However, taking a closer look, I realized they were already known to me. They were all people whom I'd met on my first visit to Tregenna. Jason Ormsby, Lord Ormsby's nephew and heir, sat collapsed in the corner of the settee like a rubber man with no spine to hold him erect. His head with its fine silvery, pale hair, drooped forward, and his arms lay abandoned in his lap like extruded toothpaste. Stella Regis, Lord Ormsby's secretary, paced by the high windows, arms folded stiffly across her waist. The glossy black hair I recalled she'd worn confined in a prim knot at the nape of her slender neck now hung long and straight half-way down her back. Clad in a clinging red wool dress, she moved nervously back and forth, black eyes flicking with a high-strung intensity from the senior to junior Ormsby. Sir Peter Ormsby, whose virtual command had catapulted me to Tregenna, stood dramatically at the mouth of the huge stone fireplace. He gazed into the flames, one hand resting on the carved breastplate beneath the mantel. The flickering light colored his features with a devilish glow and I couldn't help but draw in my breath sharply at the sight of him. I saw him in that moment as the personification of all earthly evil and more specifically as my murderer. What had Lord Hap said? That it was Lord Ormsby all those years ago who had brought about his tragic demise? What could that mean? I was drawing conclusions from total ignorance.

I turned to Lord Hap for guidance and found that he, too, was absorbed in studying the group before us. His handsome face was set in contemplation; a small muscle along his jawline bunched and relaxed and bunched again, indicating his own intense occupation with the scene. I suddenly wondered if my arrival had falsely stirred his hopes beyond possible fulfillment. I had rashly blundered upon a confinement he'd endured for four hundred years. How could I presume to unlock the answers when I couldn't even help myself?

Lord Ormsby's fingers drummed impatiently on the carved stone of the fireplace mantel. "That'll be all, Simon," he told the servant. "Just leave the tray and we'll serve ourselves. I'll have no further need of you this evening."

The old man looked up at his master through the gray bush of grizzled brows, and with a grunt, shambled to the door, closing it carefully after himself.

Lord Ormsby paused, listening until certain of Simon's retreat, and then turned to Jason. Nervously Jason pushed his horn-rimmed glasses up the bridge of his long, pale nose and sniffed as he fumbled for a handkerchief.

"*Well,* Jason," Lord Ormsby prodded his nephew. "Perhaps now you'll see fit to provide me with an explanation for your extracurricular activities. It would seem that you have found it necessary to take certain measures to line your pockets without thought to questions of legality. Is that true, Jason? Speak up, man! Or have you lost your tongue, you sniveling excuse for a human being?"

The younger man cringed against the padding of the settee, his pale lashless eyes blinking rapidly. "You've—you've got no right to talk to me like that, Uncle Peter," Jason sputtered ineffectually. "I— I—" he choked, tears welling in his frightened eyes.

"Damned bully," Lord Hap muttered.

A sharp-edged woman's voice broke into the encounter. "Bravo, Jason, my dear. Who would have thought you possessed so much acting ability." Stella Regis clapped slender hands in mock applause. The deep hollows beneath her prominent cheekbones marked a gaunt prettiness now tautly strained as she teetered on the brink of hysteria.

Lord Ormsby answered, his tone surprisingly placating. "Do calm yourself, Stella, my dear. Let me pour you a brandy to settle your nerves. This is not the time for us to be falling out among ourselves." Taking the decanter from the tray, Lord Ormsby splashed a generous portion of brandy into a snifter and held it out to the distraught woman.

Stella declined the brandy with a terse shake of her head. Turning her back to Lord Peter, she wrapped her arms tightly around her slender body and stared out the window. "I can't stand this beastly charade any longer," she wailed, her voice rough with tears. "Must you persist in this silly act? There's no one here to impress with your performance!"

Jason Ormsby opened his mouth to speak, but, watching his uncle, thought better of it and pressed his lips tightly together. The elder Ormsby merely grinned contemptuously. Swirling the brandy in the snifter, he returned it to the tray. untouched, and addressed Jason.

"Well, now, perhaps if the histrionics are over, we may get back to the original discussion, eh, Jason? What have you to say for yourself?"

Jason averted his eyes. "I—I don't know what you're talking about, Uncle Peter. Whatever gave you the idea that business was not as it should be? You're overly suspicious, that's all. Mother always said you were overly suspicious, Uncle Peter. You have no right to make unfounded accusations, no right whatsoever. And furthermore—"

A light tap sounded at the door. It opened just enough for a woman's gray head to peer cautiously around the edge. "Oh, there you are, Peter, dear. I've been looking for you everywhere. May I come in?" The intruder's high-pitched voice trailed off as she observed Jason and Stella Regis. She nodded cautiously to both of them, holding her hands behind her back in an attempt to conceal the object she was holding.

Lord Peter hesitated, apparently reluctant to have his sister join the group, but Jason immediately jumped up and drew the woman into the center of the room. "By all means, do join us, Aunt Elvina. Come in and I'll have Simon bring you some of that cinnamon tea you like so very much. That's a girl. Make yourself comfortable on the settee and I'll ring."

Elvina hung back, eying Jason suspiciously. His display of solicitude was obviously a new experience for her. She turned large sad eyes appealingly to her brother, but realizing no aid was forthcoming from that quarter, she launched her own timid attack. "He—he's here, Peter," she began breathlessly, her eyes darting expectantly about the room. "I know he's here. I feel it in my bones. The Tregenna ghost walks tonight. He's in this very room, I swear to you." Aunt Elvina looked directly at Lord Hap and smiled wistfully.

Startled, I turned to Lord Hap, who just shook his head in dismissal. "Don't worry," he whispered out of the side of his mouth. "She's just a poor daft old lady with a penchant for ghosts in her attic." He tapped his head meaningfully. "She can't see a thing where we're concerned." He nodded slightly in Elvina's direction, a gentle smile on his face. His tone had not been unkind.

Lord Ormsby's face flushed with anger. "For heaven's sake, Elvina, are you totally out of your mind? When are you going to stop this nonsense about ghosts and wailing spirits? Must I have you locked up in order to preserve my peace of mind?"

Elvina's eyes grew wider but she would not be intimidated. She held out the camera that she'd concealed behind her back. "But I have infrared film in my camera this time, Peter. You'll know I'm not mad when I have a picture of the ghost. I do so want to see his face," she said. "He's really such a nice ghost. I've come to feel that he's almost a friend." She paused, considering. "Of course the other one's nice, too. . . . He sings those naughty songs, but I'm afraid that one likes his bottle too much to carry on much of a conversation."

Lord Peter threw up his hands in exasperation and wheeled to face the fireplace, his back to the room.

Conjured by Elvina's mention, Perrigrine swooped in from some nebulous niche, alighting upon the myriad-crystalled chandelier hung in the center of the room. "Oh, I love a chesty lass, to cuddle 'mongst the grass, her head upon my shoulder and my hand upon herrrrrr . . . waist!" Swaying back and forth, he warbled gleefully. With his talons set firmly upon a glass branch, he swung over backwards, hanging briefly upside down before righting himself.

Lord Hap grimaced but said nothing.

Aunt Elvina's thin body stiffened. She tilted her head to one side, listening. "The spirits are with us, Peter," she informed him solemnly. "They're all around us, watching and waiting."

Stella uncoiled from the shadows. "For heaven's sake, stop this nonsense, you silly old bitch!" she screamed. "Shut up! Will you, you old fool? Just *shut* up!" Sobbing, Stella crumpled forward, her hands covering her face.

Lord Ormsby and Jason regarded Stella's sudden outburst with a tight-lipped grimness, but it was the elder Ormsby who immediately recovered himself and hastened to her side. "Steady, old girl," he soothed, his arm going around her trembling shoulders. "You're just tired and overwrought. A good night's rest will put you right again, you'll see. Come along, now, and I'll ring for Mrs. Figit and she'll tuck you up nice and comfy for the night. That's a good girl, Stella. Nothing to be upset about. Surely not ghosts."

Jason's pale-blue eyes slid from Lord Ormsby to Aunt Elvina and rested on the old woman significantly as his uncle led the sobbing Stella to the door. As Lord Ormsby reached for the knob, the door inched open of its own accord, emitting a chalkboard screech that sent shivers crawling up the back of my neck. Weird. Old Simon's entrance had been discreetly silent. I jumped back as the door burst open, and from the outside passage a gust of icy air rushed into the salon. Overhead a thousand crystals twittered their discordant music. Uneasily Perrigrine ruffled his feathers and muttered an unintelligible epithet, casting a baleful eye on the assemblage below.

The frosty air surged inward like a blast from a deep freeze. The lights perceptibly dimmed and the darting tongues of flame on the hearth shrank as if cowering away from the alien presence that suddenly pounced upon us. Instinctively I moved closer to Lord Hap, who narrowed his eyes as he attempted to penetrate the ghostly phenomenon invisible to us as well as to the startled people in the room.

"What is it?" I whispered. He shook his head and motioned me to silence.

A terrified scream broke from Stella as she struggled to free herself from Lord Ormsby's restraining arm. "Let me go! I've got to get out of here!" Desperation had contorted her features into a mask of terror; eyes wide and unseeing, vermillion lips twisted in fear. "I've got to get out of here! Don't you understand?" Frantically she tore away from Ormsby's grasp and ran into the outer hall, her footsteps clattering away into nothingness.

Jason started after her but was called back by Lord Peter. "Let the poor fool go, Jason! What harm can she do? *Think*, man!"

Slowly Jason retraced his steps and stepped back into the room. Smoothing his hair back with a trembling hand, he slumped into a corner of the settee where Aunt Elvina sat half crouched, her sad, ruminative eyes cast down. "The spirits are with us," she intoned in her high-pitched, sing-song voice. "The spirits are with us and they demand restitution."

I looked questioningly at Lord Hap.

"Don't look at me," he defended. "The poor daft old lady's got a misguided bee in her bonnet. Granted, there's some mysterious force present in this room, but *I* certainly can't account for it. So don't be addressing any such accusing glances in *my* direction, Lady Caroline. It's as much a puzzlement to me as to you."

Aunt Elvina lifted her face toward the ceiling. "Is there anyone here?" she whispered. "Come forward, oh denizens of the astral plane. Materialize and tell us how we may serve you."

There came another vicious whoosh of icy currents accompanied by a frenzied jingle of crystal overhead. A subdued Perrigrine clung desperately to his perch, cautiously keeping his mouth shut.

This time Lord Hap, perhaps concerned for Aunt Elvina, challenged the spectral presence. "Who goes there?" he demanded. "Who comes among us spewing his evil fear! I demand to know! Show your face that I may mark it and dispatch it back to hell!"

Thus confronted, the alien force in a last act of defiance directed its temper in a whirling gust at the maroon drapes, sending them ballooning outward. Then, abruptly as it had come, it departed. The lights brightened and the logs in the fireplace once more crackled with a lively flame.

Visibly shaken, Jason heaved a gut-rooted sigh of relief.

Lord Peter plucked spastically at his right eyebrow. "Damned drafty old places, these castles," he temporized. "Must have central heating installed one of these days."

Aunt Elvina would not have her personal ghosts so summarily dismissed. "You're wrong, Peter," she corrected in a wise, knowing voice. "What we've experienced in this room tonight has nothing to do with the heating system, brother dear. We've been visited by the restless souls from the great beyond." To emphasize her point, she dramatically flung out her arms. "Dark deeds have been perpetrated within these walls, Peter . . ."

There came a fumbled crash as the crystal decanter stopper slid through Jason's trembling fingers.

Lord Peter glanced with annoyance at his nephew and immediately returned his attention to his sister. His attitude, more conciliatory than before, bordered on the unctuous. "My dear Elvina," he counseled. "You spend too much time alone, dwelling upon the dead past of this mausoleum. You *must* realize that the ambiance that surrounds you is greatly responsible for your little fits . . . of fancy, shall we say." His voice hardened. "Now be a good girl and get yourself off to bed. There *are* no ghosts here, Elvina."

Lord Hap smiled mischievously at me.

In the face of her brother's reprimand, Elvina's fragile facade of defiance collapsed. Her face sagged; the patches of rouge on her cheeks lay upon the skin like vanquished flags. "Yes—perhaps you're right, Peter," she capitulated. "It's the voices, you know—I hear the voices and they're so very real. . . ." She allowed Lord Peter to assist her to her feet. Distractedly she brushed strands of silvery hair back from his temples. "Good night, Peter . . . Jason . . ." she mumbled vaguely, and tottered toward the door. Suddenly she paused. "I—I almost forgot my camera." She found it on the settee. "I suppose it was foolish to think I could really take a picture of a ghost," she commented to herself, "even with infrared film."

I heard Lord Hap's disgruntled snort and glimpsed his lightning movement from the corner of my eye. The camera flew out of Elvina's startled hand, rebounding off the couch and triggering the flash attachment.

While Lord Peter and Jason stood blinking, dazed by the searing light, Elvina scooped up the camera and hastened out of the room.

Chapter 4

Lord Peter closed the door firmly after Elvina's departure, leveling an accusing stare at Jason. "Now, what the hell's going on here, Jason! I think I've got the right to know!"

The younger man carefully poured another brandy, swirling the amber liquid in its glass. "I don't think you're in a position to *demand* anything, *Uncle.*" Jason's tongue rolled over the last word, imbuing it with contempt. "We're in this together, and don't you forget it." Raising the glass to his lips, he gulped the liquor. His Adam's apple plunged downward and bobbed up again under his chin. Clearly a change had come over Jason since his aunt's departure. Now he returned Lord Peter's gaze with cool equanimity.

"This is no time for squabbling in the ranks, *Uncle.* Your trusted secretary has already proven more of a detriment to this operation than she's worth. You're going to have to straighten her out before she spills everything she knows. Her hysterical outbursts are verging on the psychotic."

Impatiently Lord Peter brushed the matter aside. "Yes, yes; I can handle Stella. Don't worry about her. What I want to know is when Davis will arrive from London. Did he say he was bringing the money? The full amount?"

Jason's triumphant smile spread slowly. "Three million American dollars, Uncle. He's bringing *three—million—dollars.*" Jason enunciated the words slowly, savoring their meaning. "Not a bad price for a month's work."

"Did he agree to buy the Medici set, as well?"

Jason nodded. "He bought the whole package. The

Renoir, the Gaiadano Venus *and* the Medici set. Satisfied?"

At the mention of the Medici set I glanced at Lord Hap, raising my eyebrows in a question. He caught my meaning and nodded. The possibility of its acquisition had brought me to Tregenna. Why would Lord Ormsby offer it to me when it had already been virtually sold to another buyer? It didn't make sense unless he hoped for competitors to bid up the price. But I hadn't even been given the opportunity *to* bid. Why would he invite me to the castle and then detour my car into an early junk yard?

I found myself studying Lord Peter with a concentrated intensity as if I expected to find the answers written on his face. Several times, while he conversed with Jason, he glanced uneasily over his shoulder as though sensing my scrutiny. Perhaps Aunt Elvina's ghost stories had made an impression on him after all. I felt an overpowering urge to somehow make myself known to him. Never a vindictive person while alive, I now felt my circumstances entitled me to harass my tormentor . . . perhaps just a little. I caught Lord Hap's amused eye on me. "Women!" he admonished mildly, lifting his eyes skyward. "Give them an inch and—"

"That's not fair," I protested. "That man"—I pointed an arm toward Lord Peter—"that man just killed me! And I don't even know why! I'm only twenty-six years old! I had a great future ahead of me in the antique business and now I'm haunting this musty old dump with a four-hundred-year-old spook and a drunken parrot!" The light in Lord Hap's eyes suddenly died. Visibly he drew away, isolating his hurt in an icy cocoon. Oh, God! What had I done?

"Lord Hap . . . Forgive me . . . I—"

"You assume too much, my Lady Caroline—as you have always done," he said coldly. "No apologies are required. You are impetuous and blinded by your passions. You are intense and inflexible in your pursuits." The hatred in his voice went through me like the thrust of a blade. "I have no desire to keep you here against your wishes," he continued. "Nor to keep you under *any* circumstances."

Bewildered, I blinked up at Lord Hap's profile, turned resolutely away. How I longed to touch the crisp, black hair that grew back from the wide forehead. My fingers tingled to trace the line of the long, straight nose, to caress the short, pointed beard above the stark whiteness of the brief ruff circling his throat. I caught myself, appalled at my thoughts toward this man—a spirit that only hours ago was a virtual stranger. Distractedly I tried to focus my attention on Jason and Lord Peter. Surely they held the key to my earth-bound prison. Surely . . . Again I lifted my eyes to Lord Hap. Or . . . was it *he* who held me a prisoner within these dreary walls? Was *he* my jailer?

I tried to concentrate on the continuing exchange between the senior and junior Ormsbys. Even though they considered themselves alone they spoke in muted, urgent voices. Jason talked in a low monotone, exuding a cagey shrewdness that had emerged curiously from his previous cloak of inanity. Obviously Lord Ormsby and Jason were conspirators, but conspirators in what dark scheme—if indeed it was dark? Lord Ormsby's name ranked high within the antique collector's world, both as a connoisseur and a dealer. There was nothing patently suspicious in his selling items from his own treasure trove. And what could he possibly gain from my death? Still, my separation from life remained a reality. Someone had deliberately set a detour sign in my path; of that I was certain. If the answers were not to be found in this room, then it was time to expand my search over the remainder of the castle.

Lips parted to speak, I turned to Lord Hap.

"I know," he said, one hand raised, resignation in his voice. "Time to complete the grand tour." Apparently he'd forgiven me for my insensitive remark. At least he was talking to me again, although the warmth of our earlier camaraderie remained regrettably absent. The glint in his hooded eyes now held a subtle edge of hostility that hadn't been there before. My thoughtlessness had wounded him, or at least pricked his pride. He was willing to forgive but not forget. Was it possible that he harbored some grudge from another life for which I must bear the brunt? *Could* he harm me? No, of course not

—after all, I was already dea— The thought exploded in my mind! Perhaps he had already been responsible for my death. My eyes flew to Lord Hap's face. In this unguarded moment his handsome features swam before my gaze, stabilizing into a harsh mask of evil, forbiddingly satanic. Fear ballooned in my chest. Caught unawares, his deep-seated anger, fierce and devouring, seemed to focus upon me like a magnifying glass targeting a pinpoint of light into flame. A feverish chill went through me. There was no time to waste. I must escape this devil's purgatory or be consumed by it.

My smile was bright and toothy. "Please lead on, my lord," I said a little breathless in my deception. "I'm anxious to see Tregenna as I'm sure only you can show it to me."

The corners of his mouth curled in a faint, humorless smile as he inclined his head in a token bow. "As you wish, my lady. Shall we start with the main hall, or perhaps you would prefer the library? I believe you expressed an enthusiastic wish to spend time in the latter. You should be able to indulge your shopkeeper's passion for antiquities in either of the rooms."

I allowed the sarcastic thrust to fall unheeded.

Side by side Lord Hap and I flowed from the reception room, leaving Jason and Lord Ormsby in a hushed pantomime. The central hall was darkened now except for one timid candle drooping in its crude wall sconce. We proceeded up a flight of narrow stairs. A fugitive wind trapped in the narrow corridor howled its displeasure, dogging our path with its chill, whining harangue. Shuddering, I glanced nervously over my shoulder. It was a great night for ghosts.

Nearing the top of the staircase there suddenly appeared the silhouette of a woman, her back to the wavering hall light that cast her face in shadow. From the curvaceous outline I discerned the woman to be Stella Regis. She stood frozen, her head tilted, her eyes straining into the darkness. "Are you there?" she asked empty space cautiously. "You can trust me. Please, say something. I know you're there—I can feel it."

I looked at Lord Hap and pointed an inquiring finger at my chest. Was she talking to me?

He shook his head. "In faith, I do not know what plagues that lean one," he admitted, equally bewildered. "In all the months she's inhabited these walls, not once has she accosted me." He lifted wide shoulders in a wondering shrug. "In truth, I do not believe that she is able to discern our presence even now. Surely she has tipped her glass a time too many, warding off the damp of the storm."

"Is it Perrigrine she may have heard, Lord Hap? He certainly seems to get around this place, and even Aunt Elvina's under the impression she's been carrying on a conversation with him." I looked about expectantly, waiting for the impudent bird to make an appearance. Nothing happened. A chill current of air merely curled more tenaciously about my toes, wailing its mournful lament to the darkness.

Without warning the icy breeze scampering at our heels snarled into an angry gale. Stella staggered backwards as the whirling force struck her head-on, tearing at the pink chiffon of her nightdress and whipping long tendrils of black hair into a writhing frenzy about her terrified face. She fell back again, bare arms crossed over her breasts, and I saw the abject terror mirrored in the wide, staring eyes. "No . . . no, please, don't hurt me . . ." she whimpered. "I—I couldn't help it. He made me do it. I'll do anything you want. Anything—just don't hurt me."

As she trembled against the paneled wall, Lord Hap, unknown to the hysterical girl, leaped to her defense. Planting his booted feet firmly apart, he raised his magnificent body to its towering height and lifted clenched fists.

"Get thee gone, you sniveling coward of a dog. Do ye only vent thy miserable temper upon poor, weak women? Show thyself and meet a suitable foe."

As before, in the salon, once challenged, the whirling phantasm instantly withdrew.

"Methinks," Lord Hap spoke whimsically into the sudden void of silence, "that in all sincerity I can vouch that the devilish presence was *not* Perrigrine." A hint of humor warmed the dark eyes. "He may sink his head in a tankard at times but he lacks the imagination for real mischief."

Paralyzed with fear, Stella still crouched against the wall. The meager light distorted her features, drawing the flesh tightly over the gaunt cheekbones, sinking the eyes in shadow. Her pale, trembling lips issued a low-throated cry of terror. Jumping to her feet she disappeared down the corridor. A door slammed and was quickly bolted.

I sidled over to stand next to Lord Hap. I was impressed by his behavior but decided not to make a big thing of it. There remained the very real possibility that he'd staged the whole episode. Who better could command an errant spirit than his immediate superior? And what better way to keep me off balance and off my guard. He plays the big hero and I follow him to the ends of the earth—and fall off. Very clever.

Lord Hap looked at me oddly, and I immediately blanked out all thought. He could read me too easily for comfort, I decided. I'd have to watch that.

"And they said chivalry was dead," I quipped lightly.

He stiffened with annoyance. "Now what nonsense spills from your beauteous lips, fair Caroline? Who's this 'they' that kills chivalry, pray tell?" His jaws came together, grinding out his exasperation. "You are the most irritating woman I have ever known, Caroline. Forever chattering in riddles—you . . ." He broke off, swallowing his tirade. Anger simmering in his glance, he turned away, tight-lipped.

I suppose he'd expected me to be impressed with the noble gesture of shielding Stella. I would have been if I didn't find myself questioning his motives. The hatred in his voice suggested another, earlier relationship between us. Was it possible that he'd nurtured a grudge for four hundred years and avenged himself by sending me hurtling over a cliff? I had never believed in reincarnation, but now I wasn't sure. I'd never believed in ghost stories either. I chose to take the offensive. "Uh, tell me, Lord Hap. If that tornado that just whipped through here, terrifying Stella Regis, wasn't Perrigrine, perhaps you'd care to explain just what it *was*. You're the resident ghost around here. You should have *some* answers."

Lord Hap drew back his shoulders and raised his head, giving me a long, cool stare down the length of his aristocratic nose. The long, sensitive fingers pulled at the point of his beard. "It appears to be an eternal failing of mine," he said wearily, "to continually expect more from you than you're capable of giving, Caroline. But then . . ." He spread his hands in a kind of helpless resignation. "With a man's foolish and vulnerable eye I look upon the beauty of your face and erroneously assume that it extends beyond the mere shallow surface of your flesh. Nay, do not draw back, Caroline," he reproved softly, the censoring edge still sharp in his voice. "Like a child you wound and then recoil, shocked by the pain you inflict. And always the concern and tender regret spring as a curative balm from your lips, and so it soothes until the next occasion when your asp tongue darts and draws its blood again and again until all life flees the hapless carcass."

Lord Hap's razor-edged diatribe left me too stunned to speak. Trying to recover my balance, I realized the hard grip of his gaze had shifted and now focused beyond me, upon an infinite hole in space—and I suspected in time, as well. I spun around, calling out. "Who's there? Who were you talking to, Lord Hap? Is there someone else here? Hello? . . . Are you there? . . ." I advanced down the corridor's dark tunnel, continuing to call until, to my shocked surprise, a massive, elaborately carved door creaked open a scant six inches.

Chapter 5

"Yes, here I am," came Aunt Elvina's faltering response. "Who calls me?" The old woman's face appeared in the narrow aperture illuminated in the flickering glow of the candle she thrust a few inches through the opening. Her goldfish eyes were wide with fright and her silver-white curls trembled upon her small head. Another impatient muttering voice sounded from the inside the room and Aunt Elvina cast a quick reply over her shoulder.

"I tell you, someone called to me, Binky. You know your hearing isn't what it should be, dear." Aunt Elvina peered again into the hallway, pushing the door open wider and lifting the candle shoulder high.

My first reaction was to step back out of the yellow pool of light. A second impulse brought me directly into its brief radius. If she had heard my voice perhaps her extrasensory perception was tuned keenly enough to fully communicate with me and Lord Hap. Earlier in the salon, she'd mentioned talking to the Tregenna ghost, but obviously she'd never actually seen him. But if I *could* communicate, what then? Lord Peter and Jason would declare her a certifiable nut and probably have her confined. I did not wish that fate for this nice old lady, but I did need to talk to someone who still lived. I admitted to dying hard; even a tenuous touch with life could not be disregarded.

I thought Lord Hap was still behind me, but suddenly he stood between me and Aunt Elvina, his expression serious as he gazed down at me. "Do you think that wise, Caroline?" he asked quietly, and I realized I'd again left my thoughts unguarded.

"Wise, m'lord?" I countered. "You've already made it

quite clear that I'm less than perfect. Why would you doubt my motives now? Surely you know that they're only self-centered and grasping, as you've already judged. Why bother to ask?"

"My dear Caroline . . ." he murmured, his voice inflected with hurt and sadness. "Say no more. Perhaps . . ." He shook his head wistfully as though he brushed aside some heartfelt desire that could only die without reaching fruition. "Do as you wish, Caroline." He sighed and moved aside resignedly.

Perhaps he was right, but my course was charted and somehow I could not change its path. "Elvina," I crooned. "Elvina, it's Caroline. Do you hear me, Elvina? Please, oh, please, Elvina. Come in, will you?"

Elvina's candle froze in mid-air as she paused, listening.

A whiskered gentleman, his gray mustache bristling, popped his bald head out of the inner room from which she'd emerged. "What the devil's going on out here, Elvina?" he blustered. "Are you fraternizing with those damned ghosts again? You know what'll happen to you if old Peter hears of it, don't you? It's off to Bedlam with you, that's what. Bedlam, you hear?"

Elvina raised a cautioning finger to her lips. "Hush, now, Binky," she reproved, still listening. "You'll scare them away, and I do believe Lord Hap has brought a friend to meet me. How charming." She shifted the candle from one hand to the other and graciously extended the right one as if she expected it to be gripped in a formal introduction. "I'm so very pleased to make your acquaintance, Caroline," she beamed. "Lord Hap and I have been friends for such a long time and I know how lonely he's been. I'm so happy you've come to share his . . . confinement."

I could hardly believe my ears! Elvina heard me! She heard me!

Warily glancing up and down the hall to satisfy himself that no one witnessed the episode, Binky grabbed Elvina's arm and dragged her into the library. The high carved door slammed securely at his back.

"Elvina, Elvina . . ." he grieved, shaking his head. "What am I to do with you? Must you continuously tempt the fates, woman? Peter would like nothing better than to put you away, old girl. For heaven's sake, don't give him the fuel to build the fire under you."

Elvina patted his arm and smiled sweetly up into his ruddy face. "Binky, my dear old friend," she cooed, "what would I do without you to watch over me? I am fortunate to have such a kind neighbor. But, oh, dear! Where *are* my manners! Do let me introduce Caroline and another old friend, Lord Hap."

In the library, I stood eagerly by, watching and waiting to be addressed again. Lord Hap preferred to remain aloof, appearing at a mullioned window to glare out at the storm-wet blackness. Streams of water pelted the glass panels. Gusts of wind rattled the panes and set the long brown drapes swaying in silent rhythm.

Binky's faded protruding eyes regarded Elvina for a disturbed moment and then, pendulum fashion, he cast quick glances left and right. "Are they here now?" he whispered.

"Oh, of course they are, dear Binky," she trilled girlishly. "Caroline is standing right next to you."

The old gentleman turned his head and looked suspiciously at a full suit of armor standing three feet away.

"No, no, dear. Not over there. *Here*." Elvina pointed at me but it was obvious from Binky's puzzled expression that he didn't see me at all. With a deflating sigh the portly little gentleman sagged down on a couch, still watching Elvina with obvious concern. So only Elvina was endowed with the power to see and talk to us.

That raised another question. "Elvina? . . . Why, then, in the salon did you acknowledge our presence but claim not to see us?"

Her brow puckered. "Yes, I've asked myself the same question, Caroline, and the only answer I can offer, after discussing it with Lord Hap, is the presence of strong emotion. Emotion strong enough to generate a connecting sensory bond. I presume you were rather highly charged emotionally a few minutes ago as you came down the hall, calling?"

"Um, yes." I nodded. "I guess you could say that."

Elvina beamed. "Oh, I'm so glad, because that fact substantiates some research Binky and I've been pursuing. You see, in times of extreme duress, the substance of your ectoplasm radiates an electrically charged force field and for a short period of time you may actually sort of . . . transmit. As it happens I apparently have a natural, built-in receiver." She leaned forward. "However, in all confidence I must confess, you and Lord Hap and that funny fellow who sings those naughty songs are the only spirits with whom I've conversed."

I hid a smile. Evidently Lord Hap hadn't the nerve to tell her she'd been talking to a parrot. Keen to learn, I asked another question. "How long can we communicate, Elvina, before my, uh, battery runs down?"

"Well, I suppose it depends on how upset you are. The angrier, the sadder, the more turbulent your reactions, the greater the charge to your transmitter." She hesitated and I sensed she had a question of her own to ask. "Uh, Caroline," she hedged. "How is it that we've not met before? I'm so accustomed to Lord Hap and his friend that they're just like family. I was wondering, uh, do you plan on making a habit of whirling in and out of rooms, up and down stairs—you know, that sort of thing?"

Lord Hap moved away from the window, he and I exchanging glances. I didn't want to frighten Elvina, but quickly decided she could handle the truth. "I'm not responsible for the free-wheeling windstorms," I said. "In fact, neither Lord Hap nor I have the slightest inkling of what's causing it. If I didn't know better I'd say the place was haunted." I smiled weakly and looked to Lord Hap for assistance.

"She's quite correct, Elvina," he agreed. "We don't know who or what is behind this strange phenomenon. Merely that it's just appeared and we hope that it will disappear as expeditiously. However, that's not the reason we've come to you." He sketched the circumstances of my arrival and our suspicions, and asked for her help.

Tears of sympathy welled in Elvina's wide blue eyes, spilling down the faintly wrinkled cheeks. "Oh, my poor dear," she gasped, jumping to her feet. "We must go release you from the wreckage at once! I can't bear the thought of you all broken and crushed in this terrible rain. I—"

Binky sprang off the couch where he'd dozed off after

listening to Elvina's one-sided conversation. "Who's all broken and crushed, Elvina? Dash it all, woman, what's going on?"

Lord Hap quickly interceded. "Rushing out into the rain at this moment would serve no purpose, dear Elvina. Please calm yourself. Caroline is quite dead. There's nothing you can do for her mortal body now. *However . . .*"

Her wide eyes brimming with tears, Elvina allowed Binky to lead her to a couch and settle her in place. "Yes. Yes, I suppose you're right, Lord Hap," she conceded. "The astral vibrations have been just quivering in my chest all day. I knew *something* was happening. Yes, I *knew* it." She slanted a shrewd glance up at Lord Hap. "You said, *however,* my lord. Please finish the sentence. However *what?*"

"El—*vina!*" The frustrated Binky yelled out the name. "You've got to stop this nonsense! I don't know how much more I can take! Do you hear?" The points of his mustache bristled.

Elvina gave his hand an affectionate pat. "Calm yourself, Binky" she soothed. "Take a deep breath and relax, my dear. Why don't you just stretch out on the couch and rest your head in my lap. That's a good lad; sit down and lay your head right here. There, now, doesn't that feel much better? Close your eyes and I'll stroke your forehead. Oh, my. I can feel all that awful tension just atwitter in your poor body. Let it all go, Binky. Let all those tired little muscles just relax." Satisfied that Binky's eyes were properly closed, she continued to gently stroke his temples, uttering sweet nonsense in his ear. With a wink she signaled to Lord Hap to continue.

He grinned. "Lady Elvina, I can but say that we search for the unknown. But surely there must be some solution to our dilemma, some clue in our past history that might free us from this netherworld of existence."

While Lord Hap further apprised Elvina of our situation, what he termed my "shopkeeper's" passion for antiquities drew me away to savor the treasures displayed in the huge room. Judging by the coffered ceiling elaborately carved and gilded, I determined the library had probably been a more recent renovation by a latter-day

Ormsby, possibly within the past two hundred years. High French windows flanked one wall, opening onto a stone terrace and steps that sloped downward to a formal garden. The storm still crowded close against the castle, showing no signs of abating. Rain tapped insistently at the long panels of glass, the wind howling with the intent of blowing Tregenna down around our ears. The remainder of the wall space, floor to ceiling, housed thousands of books, many of them first editions and all beautifully bound.

Dominating the center of the room, numerous glass cases quartered a mind-bending collection of gold and silver plate; also an incredible assemblage of antique chess sets, the equal of which did not exist. Eagerly I searched for the Medici group, hopeful that it might be displayed since a buyer was expected tomorrow. I pored over each display and could hardly contain my delight when I came upon the Medici set itself. Exquisitely carved in yellowed ivory, each figure rested on a solid gold pedestal beautifully etched and set with diamonds, rubies and sapphires. Each major piece measured eight inches high, the rooks slightly smaller in stature. The tiny perfect features of the queen were supposedly those of Leonor de Medici; those of the king, her spouse, the Duke Cosimo. Golden crowns rested upon their carved heads. Totally absorbed, I pressed my hands against the glass casing and then jumped guiltily as they passed unhampered through it. I snapped erect expecting to hear jangling alarms. Nothing happened. I laughed nervously, and Lord Hap and Elvina ceased their conversation to look inquiringly at me. Under Elvina's ministering, Binky snoozed blissfully, his head still cradled in her lap.

"What is it that you've found with such happy wonder?" Lord Hap asked in an amused tone.

Elvina craned her neck carefully so as not to disturb Binky. "Ah, yes, the Medici set. I seem to recall Peter saying a Mr. Davis, a collector from Australia, was coming to bid on it. I believe he's arriving tomorrow." Elvina frowned, pursing her lips thoughtfully. "How odd." She looked at me. "Didn't you say, Caroline, that Peter called you this morning and offered the set to you?"

I nodded. *"Exactly,* Elvina, and I've been puzzling

over that situation myself. Somehow it doesn't seem logical that he'd lure me to Tregenna in order to send me crashing over a cliff." Embarrassed, I stopped, clamping my front teeth over my lower lip. "Forgive me, Elvina. I stood right here and blatantly accused your brother of murder. I—"

She waved my apology away. "Think nothing of it, my dear." A bitter little smile curved her thin lips. "After a long and painful relationship with my brother I think I can safely say with experienced conviction that he's an accomplished rogue without conscience or scruples." Elvina's expression grew distant and retrospective. "When father died he left Peter in complete control of the family fortune, mine as well as his own. My sister Meg, Jason's mother, defied him and ran off and married the young man she loved. At least Peter respected her for her courage." Elvina sighed, thinking on the wasted years. "For me, Peter knew only contempt, taking pleasure in making my life unbearable. He destroyed the only man I ever loved. Like the poor, weak fool that I am, I allowed him to manipulate me until one day I woke up and found that my life was a past tense without my ever having lived it." Elvina held her head erect, the wrinkled lids half-concealing the hatred in her eyes. "I was brought up to believe that hatred was a sin, but despising Peter has become a lifetime occupation, and I'd gladly roast in hell if I could but see him there beside me." Elvina's gaze flickered my way. "Peter—capable of murder, you say? My dear, you may have bet your life on it already. And lost. No one gets in his way and survives. Not you, not me, not anyone."

Not knowing what to say, I stared dumbly at the old woman. She'd poured out her hate and it hung now in the room like a viable entity, writhing and tortured, demanding some sort of retribution. Elvina's speech temporarily drained her of enmity, and she seemed to shrivel. The frail shoulders sagged and her head drooped forward like a wilted flower on a broken stem. I turned to Lord Hap and found him studying the Medici set, completely detached from the emotional contretemps that had just taken place.

He motioned me to his side. "So this is the famous

Medici set that brought you scurrying to Tregenna." His long fingers stroked the point of his beard. One dark brow lifted in quiet triumph and his teeth appeared white in a slow, wide grin. "Methinks, Lady Caroline, we may have come upon a ray of light in our tunnel of confused darkness."

I moved closer. "What do you mean?"

His eyes gleamed. "Remarkably enough, dear Caroline, the Medici set of which you spoke held little significance for me until I beheld it with my own eyes and then, miracle of miracles, I recognized it as the very gift I bore to the most royal majesty Queen Elizabeth all those many years ago."

I thought my eyes would pop out of their sockets. "You—you've had an audience with Elizabeth . . . *The* Elizabeth the First?"

"Aye, Mistress, the great lady herself, my good Queen Bess, who had a golden smile to light the horizon and a tongue to flay the hide from a rampaging bull." He eyed me with a roguish twinkle. "But with your woman's mind, do not be thinkin' we mingled in a lover's duet, fair Caroline. 'Twas business pure and simple, proper business of the realm."

I jerked back, startled by his accusation. Why would he think me jealous? Oddly, when he mentioned Elizabeth's name, a sharp twinge of irritation *had* shot through me. But why would I possibly care? With my chin high, I gave him my best go-to-hell regard. "It's of little significance to me what your relationship was with good Queen Bess, as you call her." I sniffed, hoping the irony of my words was properly convincing. Damn his laughing eyes!

"Ah, well, in that case, proud Caroline, you'd not be wantin' to hear the tale of the Medici set and how I, her true subject, came into the presence of Elizabeth Tudor, Queen of England."

Again, he'd made me feel like a petulant child. Mortification wriggled inside of me, but my curiosity would not be denied. "Oh, stop this nonsense," I snapped. "You know very well I'm dying to hear your story, and doubly so if it bears any relationship to our being trapped here at Tregenna." Fluttering my eyelashes outrageously, I looked up at him.

He burst out laughing and wagged a censoring finger at me. "Ah, Caroline the crafty, and not above feminine wiles when it suits her purpose. But enough of this subterfuge and on to the business at hand." For a moment he just looked at me, both question and rankling doubt in his dark regard. I'd observed that same searching speculation in his face as he'd watched me before, and I shuddered at the memory of it. He very well might be walking on my grave when he, in fact, may have dispatched me to it. Why did there always exist between us this innate need to thrust and wound? And why this feverish ambivalence that drew me so inexorably to him, only to be turned away with doubt and suspicion and lacerated sensibilities?

A muttered exclamation carried the length of the library as Binky started awake and struggled to raise himself from Aunt Elvina's lap. Still drooping over him, she pulled back, raising hands to pat her gray curls into a semblance of order.

"Deuce take it, Elvina," Binky blustered. "Didn't mean to drop off that way, old girl. Are they still here? Your ghosts?" Peering around the room, Binky swung his short legs to the floor and sat on the edge of the couch.

Elvina affected an indifferent scan of the area in which we stood but gave no indication of seeing us. I supposed my temporary field of visibility had exhausted itself. "Yes, they're quite gone, Binky," she said. "Gone . . . gone . . ." She sighed despondently, a pathetic grayness seeming to seep into her face.

Binky patted her shoulder in mute consolation and then, in a frantic effort to find a diversion, his bulbous eyes brightened. "I say, Elvina, what about developing that infrared film you exposed in the salon earlier this evening? Perhaps it may have picked up an image of your ghost. You said you strongly felt a presence. Wouldn't that be something to wave under old Peter's nose, eh? That'd put Peter Jackanapes in his proper place, that would. Come on, old girl. What do you say? Shall we give it a go?" He held out a stubby hand, palm upward. Elvina stared at it blankly for a moment and then, straightening her shoulders, she slipped her own into his.

"Yes, Binky," she said without conviction. But as she looked up into his face and read his concerned expression, a spirited little flame came alive in the large round eyes. Her voice grew strong. "Why, yes, Binky. You're quite right," she exclaimed, jumping to her feet. She took his arm and pulled him toward the door. "We've got things to do, dear. Did I tell you what a nice little darkroom I've set up in my closet, Binky? No? Well, wait till you see it." The library door swung silently closed on the departing pair.

I smiled after them. "They're sweet," I commented. "Just a couple of darlings."

Lord Hap snorted derisively behind me. "You *are* a shallow creature, Caroline," he maligned cheerfully. "Easily lead astray by superficial sentiment. How you love to wallow in sticky, synthetic emotion, wafted aloft on maudlin sighs of rapture." His sarcastic laugh irritated me and for the first time I wanted to hurt him; to wipe the smug, hateful expression from his dark, handsome face. I whirled on him, my fury searing. "Why don't you go to hell!" I screamed. "Go to hell with your meanness, pettiness and ugly tongue." I drew back, horrified by the rage I saw transforming his face.

"I need not your consignment to warmer climes, fair Caroline," he hissed through a twisted smile. "I know well the way and have dwelled there an eternity of eternities. But I am gratified to find your character consistent and to find your simpering, honeyed words still pass from a viper's tongue." He leaned his head to one side, thoughtfully stroking the fine point of his beard. "That a madonna's face should house such a traitorous heart . . ." He shook his head in wondering vilification.

Anger and frustration burned inside of me. "Why?" I begged, the hurt choking my speech, rendering the words weak and pitiful. "Why must you do this to me? Your hate hangs like venom in the air and it shrivels me. I don't understand, Lord Hap. What have I done to you that makes you hate me so? Tell me . . . Each time you loose your rage upon me I feel myself shrink and wither as though your anger devoured my very being. Oh, *please* . . ." Blindly my hands went out to him in supplication.

He turned away from me in contempt.

"Ah, dear Caroline, you always did possess a flair for the dramatic," he observed coldly, "but do not overpower me with your pathos, Lady, for I"—he swallowed hard—"I am a fool and vulnerable." A tiny muscle beside his mouth twitched, a dark sadness crowding out the animosity that seethed in his eyes.

"Why?" he asked himself as though I were not there. "Why is it that without mortal flesh, I still bleed within? Has God no pity on this feeble soul? No compassion for one of his creatures too long cast out of heaven in this nether void of existence?" He shook his head slightly.

Even as he had wounded me I could not go untouched by his misery. In all matters his pain was mine and would not be dismissed. Again I acknowledged the uncanny affinity I bore for this perplexing, infuriating man . . . spirit that hounded me to desperation and fury. I feared him, and yet the sight of his misery tore at my soul as though we'd sprung from some common source. Were we inexplicably entwined one with the other for the spiraling infinity of time? The realization left me reeling, barely capable of rational thought. And yet I think I had known from the beginning, from the time he appeared at my side by the ruins of the smoldering car, that he was not there by chance but by fate. In death as in life we shared a mutual destiny and that destiny could only be realized by the unearthly equation of the two of us, together, joyfully in harmony, passionately at odds, irrevocably joined as two searching halves seeking to be whole.

My glance fell again to the Medici set professed by Lord Hap to have been his gift to Elizabeth. Perhaps within its history there lay the ultimate key to our strange bond. It was not to be denied. Nor did I choose to deny that he and I had existed within the framework of another time. The diminutive, perfectly formed figures glowed in the murky light, casting jeweled reflections of red and blue and green. They had been participants, I suspected, in the fall and destruction of Lord Hap. I must learn their secret, for his sake as well as my own. "Tell me, Lord Hap," I implored. "Tell me about the Medici set."

Again we ranged upward, out of the library, ascending a narrowing staircase paneled in dark, ancient wood, up stone steps grooved by the footfalls of hundreds of faceless inhabitants. Had these stairs known the tap of my footsteps? Had Lord Hap's and mine sounded side by side a dozen lifetimes ago?

From the musty smell of the wide corridor, I deduced we trespassed into a part of the castle little used by Sir Peter. In silence we turned into another wing, and from mental calculations I judged it faced the sea. My guess proved correct, as in seconds there came to my ears the unmistakable roar of the waves flinging themselves on the rocks below Tregenna. An odd sensation flickered through me; moth wings of disquiet fluttering in my stomach. Did I really hear the sound of the rebounding waves? The gray stone walls were thick, muffling exterior noises. Or did I hear the memory of that sound . . . as I had once known it? I tried to swallow away the sudden dryness in my throat.

Lord Hap paused in front of a carved door that depicted a medieval hunting scene. Satisfied that I'd duly noted the fine rendering of rearing horses and raised spears, we moved through it. I decided I must be adjusting to my new life-style, because I was no longer burdened with an obsession for doorknobs.

Lord Hap and I stood in the middle of a large room which I recognized as the parlor of a suite. Two windows of leaded glass bowed outward over the cliffs, providing a magnificent view of the coast. On a clear day one could see land's end. One could . . . But again that unnerving twinge of recognition skipped across my brain. The storm obscured all but its dark insistent blur against the rattling panes. Where was the furniture? Shreds of colorless draperies still hung at the windows. Remnants of a carpet lay strewn across the stone floor. Gone were the high-back chairs upholstered in scarlet velvet and the ebony chests and table inlaid with silver. No trace of the silken French wall hangings remained. The Ormsby crest intricately worked in plaster over the fireplace mantel was barely discernible, blackened by ages of pitiless soot.

While I chased these plaguing thoughts through my mind, Lord Hap stood alone, half a room away. My fluxing perceptions had cast him in the role of a devil. Did he conjure this baffling illusion to confound me? Or did I really remember this room in its glory, secure in the knowledge that once it had been *my* room? Abruptly I turned my back on Lord Hap, not yet ready to accept that explanation. And still he held himself at a distance, proud and solitary in his remoteness.

"I don't suppose a ghost gets tired, m'lord," I said finally, not knowing how to bridge the chasm between us. At least talking would relieve some of the pressure of untenable silence.

He rested his elbow in the palm of one hand while the other stroked his beard in that familiar gesture. The face he turned to me, I was relieved to see, bore no hostility. His expression remained aloof but the hate no longer burned in his eyes. "I have not a red velvet chair to ease your weary, uh, disposition, my lady, but yon packing case may suit your purpose if you will deign to allow it." He bowed formally and gestured toward the broken box in the corner.

Grateful for ordinary activity, I seated myself, folding my hands primly in my lap.

Lord Hap stood in front of me, his feet set apart, fists on hips, his smile contrasted against the glossy black of his beard. "Ah, so docilely she sits, eyes cast down in meek submission," he mocked softly. "Can this be proud Caroline, mistress of the manor? Surely not. Who are you, fair imposter who wears Caroline's face and parades her body to deceive me?"

I glared up into Lord Hap's face and waved a clenched fist at him. "Damn you, Lord of Clowns," I snapped. "Enough of this nonsense! You brought me here to tell a story. So get on with it!" I folded my arms with adamant ill grace.

A laugh rose from his throat, low keyed and without mirth. "Very well, Lady Caroline," he humored. He half turned away and moved to the curved window seat. Settling down, he focused his gaze on the scene outside the window. I saw that the glass gave back his own reflection, yet I knew that without physical substance he could cast no shadow, reflect no image. . . . Were these images also remembered from another time? Projected from my own mind?

The storm hung suspended, now curiously without voice. Rivulets of water coursed down the multitude of panes. Lord Hap began to speak, his words slow and deliberate, plucked cruelly from scarred memory. "Set your thoughts free, my lady, and traverse with me, setting the hands of the clock in reverse. Spill away the hours, the months, the blur of years, until at last see yourself in my England of 1585. . . ."

Chapter 6

LORD HAP

April bloomed green and vital that year. Great elms and chestnut trees clad in newly donned finery preened in the golden spring sunlight. The Thames flowed placid and green, dotted with barges and ships busily trafficking its gently rolling surface. London itself was a pesthole of filth and clamoring noise, but it bore for me the magical appeal that no doubt Sodom and Gomorrah had for the young and unwary in their own day. Above all, it was home for me. English voices raised from the decks of passing ships rose sweetly on the crisp morning air. Crass and common their accents may have been, but nevertheless they were voices of my fellow countrymen. For too long foreign accents had rung in my ears. For too long had I trod hostile lands, longing for the sight of my beloved England.

Only a few short hours before, a heavily laden coach had raced along the cobblestone street directly beneath my window. Jarred by the clatter, I had bounded awake. Accustomed to awakening in a ship's crude cabin, I was momentarily confused to find myself in the unfamiliar surroundings of a homey British inn. The *Mary Regent* no longer rolled beneath my feet. The labored creak of her straining joints was benevolently absent as she nudged at anchor the home docks of London.

The voyage from the great canals of Venice numbered fifty-two entries, fifty-two days fraught with the perils such a journey promised and fulfilled. Four times pirate ships had challenged our progress, and on each occasion the sound English seamanship of Captain Cousins had sent the Barbary brigands to their respective ports empty-handed and bloodied for their thieving efforts.

Newly aroused from sleep, I relaxed beneath the bedclothes which lay rumpled beside me where the smooth-skinned bar wench had but recently vacated. The sheet beneath my hand still held the warmth of her eager body and I sighed contentedly, replete, a weary traveler whose feet again trod the soil of his homeland and whose body rejoiced in long-denied gratification. Rolling onto my stomach, I was lazily considering errands to be attended to my first day on shore when a heavy hand descended upon the door. I guessed some command lay behind that pounding fist, and hastily winding the sheet around my naked hips I opened the door. I was not disappointed. Clad in the Tudor green and white, a messenger of my sovereign Elizabeth summoned me immediately to the queen's presence at Whitehall Castle.

While the page waited below in the courtyard, I bellowed down the staircase for hot water to bathe and sharp scissors to trim my beard. As I rummaged through my sea chest for suitable finery in which to present myself to my queen, the apple-cheeked lass who'd graciously warmed my bed the previous night, staggered into the room lugging a can of steaming water. Her full breasts rounded pleasingly against the thin material of her low-necked blouse and I grinned at her reminiscently in appreciation of her night's capable labors. She feigned shyness, casting coy glances up at me through prettily cast-down lashes. On departing she giggled joyously as I spun a gold piece in her direction. Deftly catching it, she thanked me with a wanton smirk, promising future pleasures. She hastened away as other voices demanding her presence echoed in the corridor.

Properly shaved and dressed and with a parcel beneath my arm, I rode with the queen's messenger to Whitehall and was admitted circumspectly through a guarded side gate to the queen's privy garden. As I waited for the audience, I again fought to rid myself of the dreamlike unreality that pervaded my senses. It was as if the classical beauty of sunny Italy still held me in its trance. I could not shake off the haunting appeal of that once powerful nautical republic now so tragically declining in the face of the Ottoman Empire's supremacy in the Adriatic. But that was another man's war, not mine, and I was keen to report the success of my own mission. Impatient as I was, however, the quiet serenity of the queen's private garden cast a spell of complacency over me. The warm spring air was laden with the fragrance of honeysuckle and spicy jonquil mingled with the subtler scent of white roses which nodded on proud, thorny stems. The garden sloped to the shore of the Thames. Terraced on three levels, it was artfully landscaped in perfect geometric patterns laid out in boxwood and yew.

I stood viewing the river's smooth, glistening surface and the busy activity upon its face. Just below, at the water's edge, a passenger barge, elegant and brightly painted in green and yellow, drew away from the dock. I thought I glimpsed the austere figure of Lord Burghley, the queen's advisor, as he was assisted aboard. The bearded face was turned away and I could not be certain. I knew that his own estate lay a short distance away and when Elizabeth took up residence at Whitehall he regularly conferred with her, using the Thames as his means of transport.

In a few moments, two of the queen's pages appeared, carrying a gold-threaded canopy which they set down in a wide space between the garden aisles. Disappearing, they returned instantly, flanking a high-backed, red-cushioned chair which I presumed to be Elizabeth's alfresco throne. Attired in the queen's colors, the two lads positioned the chair and its dainty footstool with great care and then, casting curious glances in my direction, retired along one of the maze of paths.

In a very short time there came to my ears the sound of women's tittering laughter tinkling upon the warm, humid air. Around the hedge of shoulder-high laurel swept the entourage of my queen. I counted six fair young ladies trailing at my lady's skirts, but as they caught sight of me they halted, startled like unwary children. Their innocent shock soon gave way to knowing glances and smirks. Elizabeth dismissed them with a wave of one jeweled hand and in a second the giggling maids, heads bent as they bowed, retreated out of sight. Their exit was completed with the muffled slam of a closed door and then silence prevailed, save for the energetic buzz of royal bees impregnating the floral denizens of Whitehall.

Elizabeth never looked more beautiful to me. The sun gleamed upon her red-gold curls; her pale-gray eyes warmed to my stare as I advanced slowly, taking in the splendor of her figure. A high collar of priceless lace framed the pale, pointed face. She smiled slowly, encompassing me in her personal radiance.

I'd pledged my life to her and at that moment I would have gladly died for her, my queen, my sovereign. I sank to one knee in obeisance to my monarch, and felt the light touch of her hand upon my bowed head.

"Rise, my Lord Pettigrew," came the quick command. "Rise, my dear Lord Hap, and apprise your sovereign of your voyage to the city of islands and the royal errand upon which your queen has dispatched you."

I lifted my head to meet the penetrating depth of those cool gray eyes that I had known to darken to nearly black when stirred to anger. Benevolently now, those same eyes bathed me in their tender regard. The corners of her mouth lifted in a slight, provocative smile and the heavy eyelids closed downward, half veiling the expression in her eyes.

She turned away and with a few short steps seated herself upon the chair the two pages brought out. Arranging precisely the massive folds of her wide brocaded skirts, she then carefully cradled her long-fingered white hands in her lap. Lifting her chin high and peering down the length of her fine narrow nose, she spoke. "I've been anxious for your safety, my lord," she confided, her balance shifting to the parcel tucked beneath my arm. She lifted one finely etched brow in playful inquiry. "What is it I perceive there, so nonchalantly clutched against your person, my lord? Do you come bearing a gift for your queen?" She chuckled coquettishly, giving me a flirtatious glance.

Still poised precariously on one knee, I tore away the wrappings from the package and offered up my gift for her inspection. Resting on their bed of blue velvet, the jeweled chess pieces shimmered in the clear, morning sunlight.

Her expression did not change as she examined the individual pieces, cradling each in her hand and holding them up so the sun played upon their carved perfection. As she returned a chessman to its grooved place, her eyes bored directly into mine, and there flickered for a moment in their depths a fleeting vulnerability. Perhaps I only imagined it, for abruptly she was again my sovereign monarch. The lips that met in a straight line now crept into a widening smile and, vastly relieved, I expelled an anxious breath.

"Yes, your gift pleases me," she declared crisply with a terse nod of her red-gold head. "It pleases me because as much as you know my weakness for pretty baubles—"

I would have interrupted to protest but she held up a restraining hand. "No, no, it is true, my lord; I do have a woman's vanity that dotes upon physical adornment." She paused, again looking thoughtfully upon the chess set in her lap. "But you have seen beyond the feminine frailty and your offering suggests your acknowledgment that a brain exists under these woman's curls. God made me a divine ruler. I wish to heaven he'd made me a man as well!" Her eyes darkened with unspoken anger, and without preamble she changed the subject. "Up! Up, man!" she ordered. "Off your knees." She pushed the footstool forward with the point of her toe. "Seat yourself, my Lord Hap." She gave me a whimsical little smile. "My ego abounds when a handsome young man sits at my feet."

Elizabeth watched, scarcely concealing her humor as I squatted awkwardly upon the frail stool. And then all amusement was erased from her face, all feminine guile swept from her manner. "Tell me of Venice, Lord Hap," she ordered, lowering her voice, her cool gray eyes narrowing. "My ears are keen to learn of this new conspiracy of which your dispatches have apprised me."

Chapter 7

This was not my first secret meeting with my queen. Six months ago I had been similarly summoned to her presence. Word of my pending voyage to the Adriatic had filtered to Elizabeth's ear. Her knowledge of my journey came as no surprise; the queen's spies were numerous and well informed. Under the guise of my intended trade mission to Venice, I was to negotiate the release of a young nobleman who had ignominiously fallen into the hands of Hassan Aga, the Viceroy of Algiers and one of the most audacious and enterprising of the Barbary pirates.

The Venetian Republic, long the powerful, all-ruling queen of the Adriatic, was stunned by the harassment of the encroaching Ottoman Empire. The Mediterranean and the Adriatic seas, the undisputed Catholic domain and stronghold of Venetian supremacy, shuddered under the battering thrust of the Moslem offensive. No formal declaration was issued, but a gradual war of attrition ensued. Pirating Moslem Corsairs searched out and destroyed infidel ships. Inevitably, vessels of the Catholic monarchies bore the brunt of their attack. Reluctant to challenge English sea power, the Ottoman Empire enlisted the aid of Protestant England against Rome and its French and Spanish disciples.

Since Elizabeth's ascension to the throne, the crowned heads of both France and Spain had conspired to replace her with the Catholic Mary Stewart. Tensions mounted with each thwarted plot against the queen, while rumors of a Spanish invasion shook the British countryside. And so my sovereign Elizabeth watched and waited, hungry for news of her adversaries' fortunes upon the sea lanes. Each Spanish galleon dispatched to perdition by an Islamic galley counted as a mark in her own tally book—one less instrument of destruction that could be wielded against Elizabeth's England.

Nonetheless Englishmen continued to venture upon the perilous waters of the Mediterranean for the gain still to be realized through trade with the Levant. And should an English nobleman be captured, Moslem cupidity generally allowed for a ransomed exchange. Should the unfortunate victims be without means, their days were numbered, chained behind the oars of an Algerian galley. Upon a courier's report that young David Crichton, the Earl-apparent of Langton, languished in a Barbary prison, Elizabeth had enlisted my services as her emissary to negotiate his release. A neutral party, Giovanni di Sforza, scion of a Venetian shipping aristocracy, was to act as intermediary between the English crown and the Viceroy of Algiers, David Crichton's captor.

The wonder of Venice still pervades my mind, its wealth and grandeur too opulent to grasp other than as a fugitive from some conjured fantasy. The pink-marbled facade of the Palazzo di Sforza rose like a dream castle from the lapping gray waters of the Canal Grande. Intricate stonework fringed the graceful arches of the loggias, and the triangulated window panes flamed red in the rays of a retreating sun. In faith, I do confess to my awe at the sight of it.

A giant nubian, his shaved pate shining, ebony muscles bunching in his massive shoulders, led me up a flight of wide marble stairs into the presence of Giovanni di Sforza. The reception chamber loomed over me like a gigantic, glittering cavern. Paintings of life-size figures engaged in battle and judgment, in faith and religious adulation, covered the paneled walls. Overhead, coffered ceilings gilded with gold leaf gleamed in the sunlight, and beneath my feet, thick carpets of blood red and cerulean blue bespoke the art of Persian craftsmen.

Emerging from one of the many brocaded and inlaid chairs, the austere figure of Giovanni di Sforza stood in startling contrast to the room's vibrant color and richness. He approached, a tall, gaunt, man clad simply and without adornment in a doublet of black velvet. The only indication of wealth evidenced in his dress was the large ruby worn upon the hand he extended to me. He bowed his iron-gray head in formal acknowledgment and gestured for me to follow him into the interior of the huge room. Several high-back chairs were drawn in a half circle near a green onyx fireplace. As we neared, our footsteps echoing a hollow tattoo upon the inlaid floors, I realized that another person occupied one of those chairs, his dark acquiline face in profile as he stared into the flaming grate. I cast an inquiring glance at my host which he chose to ignore, proceeding forward, intent upon our destination.

A few feet from the grouped chairs, Signore di Sforza stopped. "Lord Pettigrew," he muttered uneasily, "it is my honor to present to you the most royal disciple of Allah, the Viceroy of Algiers, Hassan Aga."

I was stunned, but remarkably I schooled my features into calm immobility. I confronted the Aga with a passionless face that capped a breast churning with emotion. Why was he here? It obviously was not for the exchange of a mere lad of no political significance or monetary worth?

The Aga did not rise. He bowed his sleek black head briefly and I sensed his luminous eyes fastening upon my face with the tenacity of a starving leech.

Maroon velvet stretched over his wide shoulders; his black breeches were tucked into the tops of high cordovan boots. An intricately-worked gold chain holding the largest emerald I'd ever seen hung from the brown column of his neck. Laid casually upon one another, his strong and lean hands rested calmly in his lap.

I smiled to myself, aware of an adversary who weighed and measured me as a combatant upon the battlefield. The Aga's reaction came naturally, as it comes to all soldiers, and as it often came to me when I found myself mentally sparring with a worthy opponent. I gauged the Aga to be surprisingly close to my own age. From all reports of his strategic prowess as a sailor and pirate I would have expected a much older man. His hooded eyes beneath black, arched brows slid away from my face and fell to study the indifferent flames within the hearth. Our host, Signore di Sforza, hovered in the background. Now he silently withdrew, his footsteps mere whispers upon the carpeted floor.

I settled myself in the armchair across from the Aga and, folding my hands upon my belt buckle, waited.

Thunder, close and threatening, rolled across the sky. Through the long, narrow windows I glimpsed dark rain clouds, ripe with moisture, leaning ominously upon the roof tops. With another long-winded grumble, a gray veil of rain descended upon Venice, blurring the fine line and vivid color of its image.

The Aga shifted his position slightly, entwining his long fingers over his muscular chest. He opened his eyes a fraction and looked upon my face. "I think, Lord Pettigrew," he began slowly, "that we need not linger over the minor details of David Crichton's release. . . . I presume that you have been authorized to offer the amount stipulated in the original communiqué!"

I nodded once in acquiescence.

"Good! I dislike trivial details." The Aga's hands brushed lightly together, dispatching young David's life to oblivion with casual indifference.

I could not allow one of Elizabeth's subjects to be so summarily dismissed. "Yes, Your Grace, I bear the gold pieces that you have demanded and they will be delivered into your custody, but first I must see your prisoner and determine for myself that he is well and suffers no permanent damage."

The Aga shook his head impatiently, black brows raised in contempt of my temerity. "Yes—yes, Crichton is well and suffers no ill that a bath and some food will not set right. You shall be allowed to see him before the ransom leaves your possession." The dark eyes narrowed haughtily. "Do you dare to dispute my word?"

For the purpose of my mission I did not wish to challenge the good nature of the Aga. Nor did I wish to appear overly intimidated by his authority. There was no doubt in my mind that he indeed controlled the situation, but an inherent stubbornness, an obvious flaw within the fabric of my character, would not allow me to give my opponent the satisfaction of his superior position.

The Aga sighed heavily, crossing his long legs and staring intently at the toes of his boots as if his future was written there. I suspected the subject of David Crichton somehow had run its course and that in truth the

Hassan Aga now sought to broach another subject but struggled to find the proper words. Again I waited. The Aga's agitation, apparent in the nervous flex of his fingers on the arm of the chair and the quick, unconscious blink of the eyelids, set my mind to wondering. What information did Allah's most dedicated servant wish to gain or impart that ruffled the calm composure of such an exalted one? Until this moment the Hassan Aga had dominated the meeting. Now I sensed the balance of control tilt and slide into my possession.

The Aga cocked his dark head to one side and regarded me cautiously out of the corner of his eye. "I have asked that you not question *my* word, Lord Pettigrew, as a Moslem and a true believer. Now I must assume—and my intuition tells me that it is so—that you are a true subject of your sovereign Elizabeth. Is that correct, my lord?"

I started forward in my chair, not knowing what to answer. "Elizabeth's true subject?" I repeated blankly. And then the significance of the statement struck home. I settled back in the chair. "If you mean that I am a faithful follower of the Church of England, then, aye, Your Grace, you may count your premise to be true. I hold no love for the papal traitors that plot against my queen and the throne upon which she sits. Nor do I bear any allegiance to this Mary, Queen of Scots who casts covetous eyes upon England as though it were a toothsome pie for her and her supporters to divide and consume."

The air that separated the few feet between us vibrated like the twanging strings of a harp. As in France, where I'd watched the royal court energetically engaged in the new game of tennis, I sensed that I had returned the ball to my opponent. I eagerly awaited his next move.

The Aga leaned his dark head back against the plush gold upholstery of the chair and, obviously engaged in his own thoughts, gnawed upon his lower lip. Then, shaking his head as though to cast aside reservations, he said, "It may surprise you to know, Lord Pettigrew, that I possess an English wife. . . . No. No, do not widen your eyes in outraged disbelief. She is indeed my wife and would only consent to such a role after I dismissed my other wives so that she alone rules supreme within my household and within my heart." Hassan's face softened, the corners of his mouth turning up with indulgent good humor. "And but this past fortnight she has given me a son, a truly fine boy, strong of limb and keen of eye to rule after me when my bones are dust."

My puzzlement must have registered on my face.

"She was booty, my Lord Pettigrew," he stated simply. "My corsairs sank the ship which carried her to her fiancé's home in Marseille, and when she was brought before me . . . Visualize, if you will, a flame-haired beauty, skin as fair and translucent as alabaster. Eyes emerald green and flashing, aroused to fury by my assumed audacity. What a sight she was, my friend, her body so slim, so proud, defying me with every ounce of strength she possessed." Hassan's palms flicked outward in a gesture of helplessness. "It was *she* the captor and *I* the slave." The Viceroy of Algiers again sank into a pleasantly euphoric reverie as he contemplated the initial encounter with his wife.

I cleared my throat with what I hoped was a subtle discretion. "Your story is a true romance, Your Grace, but I fail to see . . ." Uncomfortably I fingered my beard.

The Aga chuckled softly, his eyes crinkling merrily at the corners. "No, of course you do not follow the confused path of my discourse. I am still bemused with the birth of my son, and its contemplation"—he shrugged—"leads me astray in my thoughts." He drew a deep breath, dismissing it through his nostrils in an abrupt rush of air, and proceeded with his story. "Much in the same way my wife came to me, certain documents recently surfaced and came to my attention. When Elaine, my wife, learned of their contents, she begged me to send a courier to your queen, Elizabeth."

At the mention of my sovereign's name I came erect and, standing, faced Hassan. "You have information regarding the safety of the crown of England, Your Grace?" Again my intuition raised warning flags in my brain. I felt certain that this prince of pirates had indeed uncovered a plot against my queen. Why else would Hassan's Elaine, an Englishwoman, seek to warn Elizabeth . . . unless some heinous plot was afoot? But the Aga would not be hurried in his tale and nodded sagely, gesturing for me to regain my seat. Without recourse I complied, sinking down again in frustration onto the edge of the adjacent chair. I bit back my impatience and waited upon the good graces of the Aga.

He stretched his long legs and carefully crossed his booted feet at the ankles. "Frankly, Lord Pettigrew," he admitted, "I care little for the welfare of England. In truth, I can appreciate your queen's position, the way she's poised as a likely spoil between the very Catholic France and Spain. And at this point in time, your Protestant England offers less of an obstacle to the Moslem world than do these papal zealots. Should Elizabeth successfully rebuff these two ravenous political powers, she would in actuality be aiding the Ottoman advance and control of the Mediterranean. . . . You fret and gnaw your lip, Pettigrew. Obviously you prefer that I get to the point, as you English say." From inside his closely fitted tunic he withdrew a packet of letters and, glancing briefly at their imprinted seal, held them out to me. "Take them, Pettigrew, and apprise your queen of their contents. When I offered my lady gold and jewels in humble appreciation for the gift of my son, Elaine refused all, and exacted only the promise that these letters be given into the hands of Elizabeth's emissary. I have now quitted my obligation." The Hassan Aga rose easily to his feet, lithe and swift in his movement.

We stood facing each other now, our eyes level. I would not have shied from combat with this powerful man but to myself I acknowledged a certain relief that no necessity existed which required our crossing swords. We were well matched, but even though I knew him to be a ruthless pirate, I could not but feel in my bones that for a few minutes during this dreary, rain-filled afternoon, a rapport had existed between us as men and as human beings. To my surprise he offered his hand, strong and sure of grasp, in farewell. Readily I accepted it.

Chapter 8

As the Hassan Aga had drawn the documents from his tunic, so now from within my own coat I extracted them and handed the packet to my queen.

For a long moment she held the small bundle of letters lightly between her fingertips, her gaze deadly upon the crest imprinted in the rosette of red sealing wax. In Venice I had recognized it instantly. Elizabeth, I realized with pity, must be experiencing that same stunned shock. I read the hurt and disappointment in the gray eyes she lifted to me, but quickly the white lids drooped, veiling her expression. With what I suspected to be a great effort, she stilled the tremor in her fingers. Resignation stiffened her backbone and set the curve of her mouth in a thin, straight line. Stoically she plunged into the business of reading a traitor's mail.

The late morning sun burned fiercely upon my bare head and I cast my eyes longingly upon the cool green waters of the Thames flowing below the terraced garden. Oblivious to the plight of mortal men and their princes, sparrows chattered among the yews and boxwood. The scent of roses filled the air, sweet and intoxicating, lulling one into a false sense of security. I filled my lungs with the garden's entrancing perfume and succumbed to its witchery as rivulets of perspiration welled upon my back and chest, meandering downward to pool under my belt. Cramped, I squirmed on the small footstool in an eternity of waiting. The heat and sounds of the garden danced in my head in a pleasant chaos of sensation, while a few inches from my ear the dry crackle of a turned page told of a present and ominous danger. Elizabeth breathed a long, painful sigh wrenched from her inner being.

I turned toward her but kept my eyes averted, not willing to crowd her raw senses at this juncture. She spoke my name in a low, choked voice I barely recognized. Her throat worked convulsively. Straining for composure, she began. "Lord Hap, you have served your queen well. I shall not forget your loyalty and allegiance. Now I must ask that you aid me once again."

"Upon my eternal soul, I am at your service in all things, Your Highness," I assured her quickly. I moved to kneel but her hand upon my shoulder pressed me back onto the stool again.

"Nay, stay where you are, my lord. We must put our heads together and deal with this situation, foul as it is." Still faintly incredulous, she shook her head.

The harsh light of the sun was not kind to her. For the first time I saw age set heavily upon her features, dragging down the corners of her mouth and weighing upon the droop of her eyelids. I wanted desperately to ease her burdens. "You have but to command me, Highness—"

"Aye, aye," she said now, frustration raging quietly in her voice. "I must *command*."

I hid a smile.

Her natural fire and arrogance, briefly dimmed, surfaced again, once more in charge. "I would be pleased to *command* my lord, if I knew just what course to follow!" A small white hand raised to tug at a bunch of curls just below her ear. She seethed quietly: "Damn, damn, damn . . ." And then apparently an idea formed, and she looked up at me with an odd, quizzical stare. "You are a bachelor, are you not, Lord Hap?" she asked unexpectedly.

I blinked stupidly, taken aback at her question. "A bachelor, Your Highness? Why yes, of course, I am unwed."

She linked her long fingers together and rested her chin upon them, a curious, elated expression alight in her eyes. "Perhaps, then, we shall have an entree into a certain seditious lair, my lord. It may just work—"

"You have devised a plan, Highness?"

Elizabeth answered my question with a question of her own. "Have you met Lord Ormsby at court?"

At the negative shake of my head she smiled slightly,

well pleased with herself. "Then most likely you've not met Caroline, Lord Ormsby's niece, either . . ."

An intuition of impending disaster swept over me.

"She's a lovely girl. Really quite pretty, heir to the family fortune, and talented upon the lute as well, my lord . . . She shall make you an excellent wife; in fact, I can but wonder why I did not think of such a match before." Elizabeth smiled with a glowing benevolence.

I had a helpless, sinking sensation in my stomach, and though my mouth was open, I found myself incapable of speech.

Elizabeth, her decision made, called for a writing table, pen and paper. The letter she composed advised Lord Ormsby of the royal resolution that his niece and ward Caroline Ormsby, be betrothed to Humphrey Algernon Pettigrew the Third, Earl of Fallingham, and of the impending visit of the future bridegroom. Elizabeth penned the notice in her artful, flowing hand, casting up amused, conspiratorial glances as she proceeded. Once sealed, she marked the letter with her royal crest and dispatched a courier to the Ormsby household.

As the garden door shut behind the departing messenger, I was consumed by gnawing trepidation. Elizabeth's eyes met mine, mischief dancing in their depths. "Do not look so stricken, my Lord Hap," she chided playfully. "You have entreated me to command you, and I have. Although I suspect you would prefer battle with a half dozen brigands than this mission that I now commend to your wit and good sense . . ." She gave a brief snort of exasperation. "If you *must* pace, my lord, then I shall pace with you." She held out her slender hand and I assisted her as she rose from her chair. In thoughtful silence, we strolled the finely tailored garden paths, each plunged into an abyss of personal reflection.

Elizabeth paused by a row of sculptured rose bushes and picked a single perfect white bud. She bent her head to draw in its fragrance, and the sun burnished gold upon her closely cropped curls. As she straightened she spoke, her mood again grave. "We are both cognizant that the letters you have brought to my attention point an incriminating finger toward Lord Ormsby. *But* if I am to take formal action against him I must satisfy Parliament with conclusive proof of his seditious schemes." Elizabeth sighed, the fine fabric of her gown rising and falling with its internal pressures. The cool gray eyes darkened with her desperate appeal. "You *must* find that proof at Tregenna, my lord."

The full circle of the path returned us to the red cushioned chair. Elizabeth's attention fell upon the Medici set glimmering in the sunlight. "Take the chessmen," she instructed. "No one save you and I knows of their existence. Include one with each dispatch so that I may know that the source is genuine." Tension eased from her distraught face as she gazed up at me. Extending her hand, she smiled slowly, again serene. "Help me to hang my enemies, my dear Hap, and forever you shall know the heartfelt gratitude of your monarch."

Elizabeth's voice echoed in my ears. Her parting words exhorted me to deliver a gift to Caroline. "Bring her a parrot," my queen ordered in her peremptory fashion. "The poor child was heartbroken when she was ensconced at court and her pet parrot perished from a chill. Surely such a gift will find its way to her heart. Although . . ."—Elizabeth tilted her head to one side, one finger tapping her cheek—"me thinks it will be your wide shoulders and manly face most likely to sway her affections." A pleased chuckle rose from her throat. "Indeed, my lord, you are the most precious gift I can bestow on any woman."

I bowed my head quickly, not wanting her to see the hot color flooding my face. Women! Barmaid or queen, ofttimes damnably contrary! Even as I made my exit, Elizabeth's shrill order was repeated in my ear. "Buy her a parrot, Hap! Be certain to buy her a parrot!"

I made my way to the inner court, where a lackey held the reins of my stallion, Zortan. "A parrot!" I muttered to myself in exasperation. Both Zortan and the servant turned to eye me curiously. "That's right!" I snapped. "You heard correctly! And unless you know *where* on God's earth I may find such an infernal creature, then I suggest you keep your raised eyebrows under your hat!" In a dudgeon I set out to find a suitable bird to present my future wife!

Chapter 9

After two days' search, I'd concluded there were no talking birds in all of London. I'd scoured the inns and pubs, the zoos and pet sanctuaries. No parrot appeared to serve my need. Despondent and disgruntled, I sat in the Green Dragon Inn, a tankard of ale between my elbows, my chin sunk upon one hand. Close to my ear, a high-pitched voice lowered an octave and said, "I heared you'd be wantin' a parrot, m'lord—and willin' to pay good gold pieces fer it, too."

It took a few moments for the words to penetrate my ale-fogged brain, but then, turning my head, I met the age-channeled countenance of a person I gauged to be a seaman. A black patch covered one eye while its mate, yellow and bulging, studied my reaction with calculating greed. A grimy red scarf was drawn over his gray stringy hair. "If that be true, m'lord, then I got 'ere whatcha been lookin' for." Without further preamble he whipped the cover from the odd-shaped parcel he carried and revealed an aged, balding, one-eyed parrot, green feathers spare and ragged, swaying unsteadily upon his caged roost.

And to think I'd given up hope! "Does it talk?" I demanded.

The seaman nodded smugly, his lower lip coming up to overlap his toothless gums. "Like a bloody schoolmaster, m'lord," he beamed.

I brought my face closer to the tiny bars of the cage. The scrawny fowl swung upon his perch, his eye closed, humming some scrap of song to himself.

I regarded the sailor skeptically. "You are positive this bird actually talks?"

The seaman tossed a small leather pouch upon the table. "I mixed 'is seed with a little sumthin' to keep 'im quiet, m'lord." The man squinched his good eye closed in a familiar wink. "Just a leetle precaution to keep 'im from making a fuss. But you'll find 'im a right chatty bird m'lord. Aye," he assured, "a right chatty bird . . ."

Was it only a week since I'd exchanged a small sack of gold for this cage that now swung from my saddle? So much had happened in the few days since I'd set foot again upon my homeland. As my retinue progressed along the road to Tregenna I found myself expecting to be awakened abruptly from a troublesome dream. Regretfully I acknowledged this was no nightmare from which I'd be aroused and could promptly forget in pursuit of breakfast. I wished that it were so. I had no desire to marry some unknown maiden even to further the cause of my queen. Elizabeth had assured me that should such a marriage transpire, and were Lord Ormsby charged with treason, any alliance with the niece would be nullified. But still the arrangement sat sourly on my conscience. Doggedly I urged my group onward to our destination.

Cornwall passed like an eerie land not quite of this world; a strange, haunted terrain its low, sullen valleys rising to the dark silhouette of jagged headlands painted with the misting purple of twilight. Certainly an apt setting for treachery, I grunted to myself.

Fatigued and saddle sore, I first saw Tregenna as day withdrew against the cloak of night. I would have preferred to arrive in the mid-afternoon with the sun as bright witness to our intrusion. Fortune that governs the lives of mortal men saw fit that it be otherwise. I was mounted upon Zortan, followed by Cedric, my valet, and the coach carrying my possessions, as we wound our way up the path. The forbidding castle reared its silhouette against the fading gray of the day. Encroaching upon it was the star-studded sweep of night, silver winking in a blue velvet sky.

At the castle gate I dismounted. A faceless servant materialized from the shadows to take my horse, but no word of greeting passed from his lips. Light shone golden from the narrow windows, but no host stood upon the stair to acknowledge my presence. Had I expected otherwise on the basis of Elizabeth's peremptory decree that the young lady of the house marry a total stranger? Were

I to find less than open hostility then *that* would have surprised me.

I made my way up the wide steps and as I raised a fist to sound upon the heavy, nailed door, it swung noiselessly open. A woman's slender silhouette stood outlined in the arched doorway. Candles on the wall behind her cast her features in shadow so that she, too, appeared a faceless minion, mere flesh and bone, to receive us and direct my footsteps to shelter and rest. My body ached with the thump and thrust of two hundreds of miles upon Zortan's able back. Half consciously I realized I still clutched the parrot's cage in my hand. Ill temper made me jolt the cage with a vicious shake, but other than a drugged groan, no sound issued from the covered shelter. The bird slept on and I envied its aplomb. The tall figure of the woman, whom I assumed to be the housekeeper, lead me up the wide central staircase of the castle. At the landing, corridored wings swept to the right and the left, long avenues stretching into darkness.

Without a word she led to the right and past several doors until, stopping at one, she turned the knob to admit us. A bright fire danced upon the hearth, shedding its cheer over the large room, casting vibrant light upon a canopied bed and solid furniture suitable to serve a man's need. I was relieved that I'd not be subjected to the white and gold delicacy of stylish French design so popular in the salons of London and Paris. I, a simple man, preferred but the basic necessities of life. It occurred to me, with a jolt, that should I acquire a wife, those tastes would vary with *her* whim.

My own home in Dorchester came alive in my mind, but I thrust it away. My duty lay here and personal preferences must be set aside. Blankly I stood in the middle of the room, a sleepwalker befuddled by strange surroundings. The confounded bird cage still dangled from my fingers and I slammed it down on a sideboard, sourly content to shake the feathered occupant from his lotus-laden sleep. The creature stirred within his covered space and, grunting, much like a human, immediately fell silent. I presumed it lapsed again into dreams. I'd nearly forgotten the woman until she spoke behind me.

"Is that a parrot housed in that shrouded parcel, my Lord Pettigrew?"

I turned slowly, leaden with my own fatigue, but spurred by the quick interest in the young voice. "Aye, ma'am, tis a gift for the Lady Caroline. Perhaps you would dispatch it to her with my warm regards and those of her queen and spoken friend. Elizabeth waxes poetic upon the wealth of her charm and—"

"Aye—and the wealth of her dowry as well, I presume," came the dry rejoinder.

Surprised by this undisguised impudence. I garnered a closer look at the young woman so brazenly exchanging words with her better. The warm firelight played upon her finely carved features, igniting sparks of color from the golden hair, which was swept back over her shoulders and fell to a narrow waist easily spanned by a man's two hands. Her shadowed eyes looked upon me with an amused contempt that I would have tolerated from no man. Into the pool of silence deepening between the woman and myself intruded the rude shufflings of the parrot.

The girl now hurried forward, all concern for the bird. "Oh, the poor creature is ill, my lord. Do remove its cover so it may be revived by the warmth of the fire. It has suffered an arduous journey from London." A decanter and glasses sat upon a small table at the bedside. She moved toward it, saying, "Perhaps a bit of brandy will warm its parched gullet and breathe life into its feeble limbs."

I might well have said the same of myself but this female, while zealous on the bird's behalf, cared little for mine. A disturbing truth lurked at my mind's edge and I braced myself, prepared for another rude shock. Drawing down my crumpled weskit with some modicum of dignity, I straightened to my full height. "To whom do I address myself, madam? Apparently I have presumed upon your identity and I would know your position in this household. Again, ma'am, to whom do I address myself?"

The young woman bent forward, crooning senseless tidings to the awakening occupant of the cage, her golden hair falling across her face like a shimmering veil. Slowly she righted herself. Amber eyes, clear as Castilian sherry, looked upon my face and mocked my mortal manhood. "I am Caroline Ormsby, my lord," she answered, silent laughter frozen in her words. "Would you have expected to be greeted by other than the lady of the household? And, indeed, that woman no less than your designated bride?" Caroline sank forward in an exaggerated bow of deference, the gesture betrayed by the sardonic smirk upon her beautiful mouth.

For my bride, Elizabeth chose for me a minx as well as a traitor. I must tred a cautious path at Tregenna, I reminded myself. This Caroline menaces my being, but not with physical peril. 'Tis the lush curve of red lips, and breasts, soft and rounded against the blue fabric of her gown, that disarm me. I moaned silently to myself, aware of my own frailty. Caroline Ormsby, I feared, could well snare me like a trained monkey upon her crafty woman's leash.

She rose slowly from her obeisance, the insolent smile still curving her lips. "Well, my lord and future master, have you no words of greeting to beguile my womanly senses?" she challenged pertly. "What? No flowery declaration of undying love, Lord Pettigrew? Surely Elizabeth has awarded me to you for some worthwhile service rendered to her. My coffers are gold filled, and I . . ." The sherry-colored eyes suddenly brightened with unshed tears and Caroline turned abruptly away. Concerned with my own discomfort, I selfishly had not considered hers. With a few brief hours' warning, a bridegroom had been thrust upon her, and she as chattel and possession was expected to share my bed and fortunes for the remainder of her natural life.

Sympathy warmed me to her. She tensed as my hand touched her shoulder. I wished for a glib tongue but merely gulped back awkward silence. "Indeed, Lady Caroline," I finally managed, clumsy as a schoolboy, "were you base born and without wealth, still princes would covet you and thrill in the splendor of your beauty!" I stopped aghast. Had those sugary phrases passed from *my* lips?

Caroline's shoulders shuddered under my hand. Frantically I searched my brain for some means to comfort her when I glimpsed the quarter profile of her face and realized with a start that laughter, not tears, contorted her features. A low chuckle curled in her throat as she twisted away from me to stand with her back to the open hearth. "Tell me, Pettigrew," she asked dryly, "was that pretty remark extemporaneous or did you compose that silly drivel in transit to sway my girlish heart?"

Stung to retaliate, I mimicked her stance, jamming my fists against my hips. "Aye, lady," I jibed. " 'Twas all that occupied my mind as I traveled hence. Empty words to woo an empty head." I reached for the bird cage and pulled off the sheltering cloth. "And I've brought you a companion to match your intellect. I hope that he may broaden the scope of your erudition."

I've often uttered careless words, much to my helpless chagrin, but never were they as lamented as that particular pronouncement. They hung in the air for but a breath when the parrot opened one jaundiced eye and bawled: "To bed, wench! To bed, me beauty! Perrigrine'll tickle your fancy! Aye . . . Old Perrigrine'll—" In all haste I recapped his cage and then with a sheep's face decided to brazen out Caroline's fit of laughter.

She mopped at her eyes with a corner of her scarf. "Pettigrew," she gasped, choking down an errant giggle, "I have not yet decided whether you are a mere victim of some misbegotten prank or a cagey wit with a perverse and delightful sense of the ludicrous. Somehow I do not think you a fool." With both hands she smoothed back the long bright hair from her flushed face. "But whichever the case, I somehow find myself more kindly disposed toward your presence at Tregenna. Had it not occurred to you previously, may I say now that the announcement of my . . . *our* betrothal came as a blow, and one from which I yet reel. Since the news arrived so unexpectedly, the lord of the manor is not in residence. Private business necessitated his travel north to Devon, but early this morning I dispatched a servant to retrieve him as soon as humanly possible." She paused and sighed. "Had he been here or had I been allowed some brief period of time in which to adjust to this disturbing situation, then perhaps I might have received you with less animosity." Caroline thoughtfully studied her clasped hands, the knuckles white with strain.

In two strides I stood before her, and without thought of propriety I placed my hands over hers. "Do you love another, Lady Caroline?" I asked quietly, dreading to hear the answer. "Because if that is so, I can doubly feel for your predicament and I shall do all in my power to ease your burden." The tips of my fingers raised her chin and she looked deeply into my eyes, searching, still apprehensive and troubled. Her pain turned a knife in my vitals as though it were my own and I told myself I must look away or fall under the spell of such eyes. Had I forgotten the reason for being at Tregenna? What if she were but a dupe who charmed me with calculated deception? If Ormsby was indeed an enemy of the queen, would he not be suspicious of one so obviously allied with her sympathies? I drew back slightly and willed my features into an expression of impassiveness. I felt Caroline's response and saw the slight quiver of her lips. Then, sensing my withdrawal, she, too, recoiled, the sherry eyes hardening with a cool glint. "Ease my burden, Lord Pettigrew? Such a task would require that you turn your back on Tregenna and retreat your steps to Whitehall."

I was still holding her hands, but now I thrust them away. This proud, haughty woman affected me as no other ever had. But I could not allow her to suspect the power she held over me. She drew me as a magnet draws base ore. Yet even as Caroline's beauty stirred my blood, I knew that I wanted more of her than the satisfaction of momentary lust.

"Come now, my lady," I reproved mildly. "You are not a child. You are fully aware of the protocol governing the gentry of this land. *None* may marry without the sanction of Elizabeth and she has seen fit not only to sanction, but to decree, this union. She bears a sincere affection for you, Mistress, and I believe our betrothal originated in her true desire to see you happily situated." My conscience struggled with the lie and subsided meekly in the face of duty.

Caroline's head came up sharply, the eyes glittering with barely contained anger. She hissed out: "And you, my lord? Are you to bring this illustrious gift of happiness to this abysmal old maid? Is your ego so inflated that you are convinced that heaven lies within the circle of your manly embrace?" She threw back her head, showing perfect white teeth, and laughed in contempt. "You flatter yourself, Pettigrew. Elizabeth's wishes be damned; I would not have you for a stable boy." She flung the words at me defiantly, and with hands on hips, cockily awaited an answer.

"Hmph!" I grunted, hoping my disdain was convincing. "I thought this wench a prize." I set my elbow in the palm of my hand and stroked the point of my beard. "And I find that she is indeed—unhappily—a *booby* prize! What could I have done to incur Elizabeth's wrath that she would burden me with such a viper-tongued wife?" Fanning Caroline's growing rage, I cast a slow, appraising glance over her figure, starting at her toes, advancing upwards and falling again to her hem, shaking my head in disparaging wonder. "Indeed, Caroline, I must concur that in truth you *are* an abysmal old maid. Methinks it is gratitude that should spring from your slitted tongue, and not foul venom. What age have you, Caroline? Nineteen or twenty summers, at least, I should judge. Quite past your prime. You should be grateful that your queen has taken pity upon thy solitary state and seen fit to provide you with a mate when obviously you have not been able to secure one for yourself." Watching Caroline's wrath flame her cheeks, I fought to control the straight line of my mouth. "However, I am bound by my queen's command to take you to my bed and make a woman of you." With raised brows I pursed my lips and studied the carpet, righteous duty plain upon my face.

Caroline flew at me, fists raised, eyes dilated in fury. "How dare you!" she screamed.

I seized her wrists before her fists could make contact and forced her arms behind her back. She struggled, captive in my embrace, her face mere inches from mine, her breath coming in quick, dry sobs. Her round, full breasts thrust against my chest. Desire heated my loins and dimmed everything but the sight of her beautiful face, eyes widening in sudden awareness of the passions mounting between us. The golden depths of her eyes held me mesmerized and as her lips parted, my mouth came down upon their sweet red moistness, capturing me in a mindless vise that only the total possession of her body would release, flesh upon flesh.

Frantically she thrashed against me, her head turning from side to side, but I would not, could not, release her. My lips held hers until she stopped fighting and whimpered, a low-throated sigh. Standing on tiptoes, she wrapped both arms around my neck, her hands cupping the back of my head, drawing our bodies even closer. Caroline . . . There was only Caroline. Her name pounded in my brain, as much a part of me as the blood coursing through my veins. Caroline . . . A searing pain burst in my mouth and, startled, I stepped back.

Like a wild animal she twisted away, and running to a small inlaid desk, snatched up a small dagger. Grasping it tightly, she held it poised as though she'd willingly plunge it into my heart. I tasted the salt on my tongue and felt the blood in a warm trickle oozing from the corner of my mouth. Instinctively I started toward her but halted as she jabbed the glinting blade at me, carving the air in a small threatening circle.

"Stand back!" she warned through clenched teeth. "Stand back, or . . . or . . . I'll kill you—I'll . . ." Tears spilled down her cheeks, choking off her speech.

I removed the knife from her unresisting fingers and tossed it on the desk top. Then without thought, acting only on instinct, I gathered her into my arms, holding her close, my cheek against the silken hair, content to shelter the trembling body with the warmth of my own. "Hush, now, Caroline," I murmured. "Hush and calm yourself. Foolishly I've frightened you. It was not my intention that we should meet in such—such a physical manner. You are much too lovely to fling yourself upon a man," I admonished softly, "and not know what desires and passions you arouse."

Caroline stirred within the circle of my arms and lifted a tear-wet face. A watery smile faintly turned up the corners of a tremulous mouth and she gulped as a mischievous gleam crept into the amber eyes. She pressed shamelessly closer, her arms snuggled around my waist. "Do I . . . uh . . . um . . . does my nearness *really* arouse you to passion?" she asked. She peered up into my face, wide eyed and serious.

She wore a woman's body and yet I suspected she had not known its physical gratification. A deep sigh ached in my chest and I felt old for my thirty-one years. I tried to free her arms from my waist but she clung contumaciously closer. I knew I must free myself or answer to the consequences of my own vulnerability. Sweet Caroline tempted me with heaven, but the face of my queen stood between us. I assumed a haughty pose and gazed imperiously down the length of my nose. "Indeed, Mistress," I reproached crisply, "methinks you are much too bold a piece. Your behavior in fact is quite brazen. One can but conclude that your habits are less than pristine."

Shocked hurt clouded the light in her eyes, and her eyelids, fringed with dark lashes, fell like a curtain over her humiliation. Her arms dropped to her sides and in vague confusion she backed away, unable to look at me, her cheeks burning red. To inflict such pain tore at my heart and in that moment I would have gone to her and begged mercy had not the clatter of hooves sounded in the courtyard below. Voices called out sharply in the night, echoing from the castle walls, and in my distracted state I did not immediately register that the language they spoke was not English but French.

All color drained from Caroline's face as she stared in consternation at the doors leading to the balcony. Compelled I went to them and, pulling them open, leaned over the parapet to more closely observe the new arrivals. A half dozen lackeys holding torches aloft lighted the scene. Macabre shadows licked at the walls like an accompanying band of silent demons. I suspected that had Lord Ormsby been in residence he would not have given me a room with such ready access to this courtyard. The thought eased my heart. Perhaps Caroline was not involved in the plot against Elizabeth, as I had dreaded. But the respite was brief, for Caroline, so close that the gleaming strands of her hair splayed upon my sleeve, also leaned over the stone railing and called what rang to my ears as a circumspect warning. "André! André! Here I am on the balcony above your head! Look up! We have a guest! Sent from Elizabeth! We are honored, are we not? He comes from Elizabeth, our queen!"

I counted thirteen men in the small troop that was dismounting and unsaddling its animals. They were dressed as peasants in crude homespun jerkins but moved with an undisguised military bearing. Though no orders were issued, they deported themselves with such precise efficiency that there was little question in my mind. Ormsby had assembled a secret army, and a French one, at that.

A chill breeze from the sea sent a shiver up my spine. My position at Tregenna grew more tenuous by the moment. However, my first concern was to gather information and send word of it to Elizabeth. I had to learn in what manner Ormsby intended to deploy his army.

Caroline still leaned over the railing, her skirts entwined with my legs, the curve of her cheek close to my eye. If there was any escape for me, I doubted I could leave her behind. I shook the traitorous thought from my mind and set my attention upon the man, André, to whom Caroline had addressed herself and with whom she now bantered flirtatiously.

He sat a fine black gelding that skittered and pranced beneath his firm, controlling knees. I must confess to immediately detesting the man, both for his handsome bearded features and for the easy familiarity with which he conversed with Caroline. Fervently I hoped that when he stepped down from his steed, his height would measure that of a midget; but as he did so, I saw, alas, that my wish was futile. Not equal to my size, he was nobly built with broad-set shoulders, a lean waist, and muscular legs encased in somber hose. He swept aside his plumed hat in a courtly bow. "We welcome you to Tregenna, my Lord Pettigrew," he said graciously from below. "But better still, allow me to welcome you with good French brandy and a warm fire at your back. May I suggest, my dear Caroline, that you direct our guest to the parlor, where we may become acquainted without the need of shouting?" He bestowed upon her a wide, gleaming smile, calculated to charm. Then, turning, he strode into the shadows and, I presumed, into the castle itself.

Silently, her eyes cast down, Caroline stepped from the balcony back into the chamber, with me at her heels. I could not restrain the question: "Who is this person so comfortable within your household who bids you to your duty as hostess, my lady? I know that your uncle is a grizzled man of many years. So who—" I broke off uncomfortably, prodded by a disquieting thought. Was this André her lover, if not in the carnal sense, then he whom she loved?

Content she'd served proper penance for her earlier transgressions, Caroline scorned my question. "You are not yet master of this house that you may demand explanations of its occupants, my lord," she said in clipped tones.

A firm tap on my door brought Cedric, my manservant, into the room, hoisting a bucket of steaming water.

"Bathe away the tiresome dust of your journey, my lord," Caroline instructed officiously. "We will talk again in the parlor." And with Perrigrine's cage hooked securely over her finger, she swept out of the room.

I allowed a pent-up sigh to rush from my nostrils. I'd done battle with a cyclone and would certainly never be the same again. Slowly I unbuttoned my weskit as Cedric poured a billowing stream of water into the round wooden tub.

Chapter 10

I contemplated my kneecaps as they rose like mountain peaks from a sea of bubbles. Cedric's voice sidled in among my gloomy musings. "Shall I wash yer back, m'lord?"

"Aye, Cedric, swab it down. The red dust of Cornwall settles between my toes and grates between my teeth. Give it a scrub." Cedric's bald head bent to the task. It was soothing to wash away the grit of the journey. I could but wish to wash away the imprint of Caroline as well. The impression of her small fists still burned upon my chest and my body hungered for her touch. Touch? Hell's fires! It was not her touch that I wanted, but total surrender! I must think of other matters. If I dwelt much longer upon that toothsome wench, Cedric would need be toting ice water to cool my ardor.

Unceremoniously Cedric dumped a bucket of steaming water over my head. "Aye, that be a peppery dish ye be takin' to yer bed, m'lord," he observed dryly. "She whushed by me like a wintry breeze off a snow bank, she did. All fire and ice, that one, and a man never knowin' which it'll be." His amused gaze narrowed, one corner of his mouth lifting in an obscene smirk. "I was thinkin' you were a bit flushed in the face, m'lord, wi' yer manhood bulgin' in yer breeches, leapin' to be at 'er."

I heaved a silent groan but could take no offense at Cedric's familiarity. My earliest childhood memory was of this paunchy old man with the watery blue eyes carrying me upon his shoulders. In later years it was he who taught me to ride and wield a sword. I suspect my mother, Elsbeth, had commended me into Cedric's keeping when she knew her death was imminent. My father never forgave me for weakening her health at my birth, causing her an infirmity from which she never recovered. At the age of five I remember standing shivering in the small stone chapel of our Dorset estate as her remains were interred in the family vault. It was Cedric's big hands that clasped my small cold ones that day. And forever after he had been to me mentor, mother, father and friend. In his grief and bitterness my father withheld from me all affection and attention one might expect a parent to bestow upon his only son. During holidays and on my birthday he perfunctorily assumed the proper role, but otherwise he engrossed himself in the management of the vast estate to which I was heir. Affectionately my regard rested upon my old servant. "What news, Cedric?" I quizzed. "Are there any sights below stairs to set your soldier's eyes to wondering?" He handed me a towel and I stepped out of the tub, drying myself and wrapping the cloth about my waist. He handed me hose as I buttoned my shirt.

"Well, m'lord," he drawled, rubbing the back of his neck, "I didn't see nothin' to put my finger upon, but this place does give me an oddsome feelin'. Nothin' I'd write in a dispatch to 'er 'ighness, but just a prickly feelin' chasin' up and down m'backbone and leavin' icy tracks." Wrinkled eyelids drooped, almost covering his eyes completely. "Somethin's goin' on here, I'd swear, m'lord, and I'll be a sly shadow in every nook and cranny of this here Tregenna to learn just what scheme abides in this pile o' rocks. See if I don't. Jist you see if I don't, m'lord."

"Good man, Cedric. I knew I could trust you to be my eyes and ears, but be cautious. Only a few minutes ago a contingency of men arrived dressed in the coarse clothes of peasants but speaking French and conducting themselves in a most military fashion. I suspect that Ormsby is forming a secret army here at Tregenna and when the time is right, most likely as King Philip launches his Spanish fleet against Elizabeth, he will launch a simultaneous offensive from the rear. There are many Catholic Englishmen who will rally to the Papist standard, Cedric. We must learn the strength of this force and, if possible, the actual plan itself."

The old man shook his head mournfully, staring blankly at the floor. " 'Twas a sorry day when tha' Mary, Queen of Scots landed on our shores, m'lord. She an' that schemin' bunch o' 'ers allowed no peace in this land since she set foot. She'd o' had the Queen's 'ead on a plate fer certain—if the luck'd been wi' 'er and a stalwart army at 'er back as well."

Cedric held out the red velvet jacket I'd bought in London to woo the Lady Caroline. I thrust my arms into the sleeves, glancing over my shoulder at my friend. "It's a dangerous road we tread, Cedric. Are you with me, lad?"

He grinned with amusement. "Lad, is it, yer callin' me, m'lord, when I dangled you on m'knee when you were a mere slip of a tadpole."

"Enough, Cedric," I commanded sheepishly. "But heed my words and take no chances. I'm certain we'll be watched like hawks so we must be doubly devious."

The old servant grinned toothily. "Aye, m'lord, if it's devious you be wantin', then I'm yer man, awright. If I not be here when you return from yer supper, I'll be down on the beach givin' a look about the place. There's a bright moon and I'll not be needin' a lantern. I'll just flit among the shadows like a bloody Cornish spook." His roguish grin spread over yellowing teeth.

"Flit if you must, old man," I cautioned, "but those are French shadows, remember, and they have sharp teeth. If they bite, they'll eat you up and spit out your miserable bones on the slimy rocks. If you're discovered, 'tis my death warrant as well."

"Aye, m'lord," he answered dryly, touching his hand to his forehead in his own version of a salute. "Me stomach prefers that my throat stay intact and not be gettin' itself slit, especially by any o' those Frenchies." Giving me a knowing wink, he turned on his heels and left the room, closing the door after himself.

I was still staring at the shut panel when a light tap sounded. I stiffened apprehensively. Had someone in the darkened hallway been listening to our conversation? "Who is it?" I demanded.

"It is I, Caroline, Pettigrew, come to personally escort you to the dining chamber," came the muffled voice.

"Open the door . . . or are you still indisposed, m'lord? If you require another pair of hands I shall send a servant to attend to your needs." She spoke slyly and I recognized her attempt to aggravate. For all her innocence, in a woman's fashion she knew the needs I had which no servant could fulfill.

I swung open the door and caught my breath. Caroline stood framed in the doorway, dressed in amethyst velvet, the low-cut neckline swelling tautly over the glorious mounds of her breasts. The rich fabric wrapped her body lovingly, hugging every curve in a close embrace. Her sun-gold hair was braided and drawn up in a perfect crown at the top of her head, although I would have preferred the splendid veil of hair to be set free of all fetters, spilled upon a pillow in impassioned abandon. Her eyes seemed to read my thoughts, and her red lips tilted in a siren's taunt. She held out her hand to me, wide sleeves falling away from slender arms, fingers devoid of jewelry. "Shall we go, Pettigrew? Dinner grows cold and our guests heat with the wait."

Her hand upon my arm, we traversed the dimly lighted corridor. I strove to keep my eyes straight, but their recalcitrant gaze refused to focus on anything save Caroline. An incredible heat seemed to radiate from that wondrous, sensuous body at my side, and the exquisite animal scent of her filled my nostrils. She drew me and consumed me, reducing all other matters to small signficance. At the same time she frightened me, her power over me too devastating to comprehend. Yet as I felt myself pulled into her web, some small vestige of reason held the moth from the flame. Duty lay as a final barrier between honor and total surrender. I'd sworn fealty to my queen, and even this overwhelming instinctual drive could not erase that onus from my conscience. I looked upon Caroline's warm, lithe body and hardened my resolve.

At the bottom of the central staircase Caroline paused. A shadow seemed to darken her lovely features, and blinking in a disturbed manner she raised anxious eyes to mine. "My Lord Pettigrew, do not linger in this house," she beseeched. "There can be no marriage between us. Accept my word and do not tarry. You can only bring disaster upon yourself. Please leave before my uncle returns, m'lord. I know you suspect my motives in this matter, but in all reverence I supplicate that you leave me and return to London. Do it this night. Tell Elizabeth that I refused your suit—oh, tell her anything, I do not care—only get thyself gone from this place and never look back!"

Caroline's passionate entreaty puzzled me. Did she still play her games or was this a true warning that danger crouched within Tregenna and I was its prey? Both encounters with Caroline had embroiled me in this same turbulence, this emotional seesaw of doubts and suspicions. I gained pleasure in hoping that she might care to warn me if I *were* in jeopardy. My only real comfort rose from the knowledge that as Elizabeth's representative, Ormsby would be loath to do me bodily harm. Harm to me drew attention to him and to Tregenna. Desperately I hoped Lord Ormsby and his cohorts still labored under some doubt as to the genuine reason for my presence. Clinging to that tenuous thread I dangled over a pit of vipers.

Transposed against these rioting images, Caroline's face reflected an inner demon of her own. A small frown stroked the fair brow and distractedly she gnawed at her lower lip. "Well, Pettigrew?" she insisted, exasperated at my silence. "Have you lost your tongue, man? I have enjoined you to leave this place and you stare as though I speak in a foreign tongue and you do not comprehend my words." She stamped her foot angrily, fists clenched in frustration at her sides. "Damn it, Pettigrew," she flared. "What must I do to move that mountainous hulk of yours? Set the dogs on you?" Her words burst out in thinly disguised anger, but verged on tears.

I opened my mouth to answer when tall doors across the hall were flung open and a man's silhouette stood framed in the oblong rectangle of light. "Ah, my dear Caroline, I feared your impulsive suitor might have abducted you and fled to the hills." André, the cavalier who'd greeted me from the courtyard earlier, chuckled softly, amused at his own wit.

Beneath my hand, Caroline's arm tensed at the intrusion. Shrugging away my touch, she sauntered toward the Frenchman, and with a chameleonlike change drew back her lips in a provocative smile. "Forgive me for lingering, André, my dear," she purred smoothly, "but I've been attempting, to no avail, to convince Lord Pettigrew that his presence is no longer required here. But by God's blood, he's dense! He refuses to accept my open declaration of undying love for you!"

Standing in the half light, André's mobile features did not change expression. I silently complimented him on his remarkable control. I was certain that Caroline's announcement came as a surprise to him as much as it did to me. I did not doubt the possibility of their being lovers, only the likelihood that she'd make such a flagrant statement in the presence of a stranger. I credited the volatile Caroline with greater subtlety than that.

Mentally I applauded André's equanimity as he countered: "To know you is to love you, beautiful Caroline. All men who set eyes on that face must succumb to Cupid's arrows."

Voicing a coquettish laugh, Caroline entwined her arms with his. "And you must know why I love you when you lie so prodigiously." Her eyes laid their full barrage upon him and he retaliated with a smitten lover's sheepish grin in return. They played the scene convincingly. Jealousy clawed at my vitals and I wished to strike his arms from hers, to wipe the insipid expressions from their faces. I drew in a sharp breath. I must think with a clear head. I could ill afford judgment befuddled by emotions such as I was experiencing.

"Is that a haunch of venison I smell turning upon the hearth, Lady Caroline?" I inquired coolly. "Its aroma stirs my appetite, and with your permission I would be pleased to dine now."

Caroline reluctantly tore her regard from André's face. "Oh—oh, yes, of course, my lord. How lax I am in my duty as hostess. Please come forward into the dining chamber. Ah, yes, I see that Count Velasco has preceded us and already waits our coming."

At our entrance, a small, serious-faced man with wispy black hair combed over his balding head stepped back from a window. His dark eyes flitted from Caroline to André and returned to her as she offered introductions.

"Lord Pettigrew, may I present Count Velasco, a dear friend of my uncle."

The count bowed stiffly, muttering some platitude.

"Lord Pettigrew has been sent by our benevolent queen to remedy the ill fortune of my maidenhood, dear Velasco," she informed him gaily. "I beg that you be polite to him since I have been so shockingly rude."

Velasco's Adam's apple dipped and rose convulsively as he brought a vague smile to his thin lips. Words lodged in his throat and he choked on them pathetically, flinging a pleading glance at Caroline. Obviously still disturbed he drew a silk handkerchief from his somber tunic and mopped at his shining forehead.

Caroline effortlessly issued another false laugh, calling attention to herself. "And not to diminish a wondrous jester's gift, let it be known that Lord Pettigrew has brought me a prodigious surprise. A parrot, no less, dear friends, can you imagine? A remarkably educated bird with an extraordinary vocabulary of a specialized nature." She grinned wickedly. "I can but wonder where our illustrious guest must have acquired his own education. Ah, but enough of this banter. Come, gentlemen, seat yourselves and let us begin the meal. I thought perhaps my uncle would arrive in time to join us but I fear he has been delayed along the road."

We entered a smaller accommodation just off the great hall. Its proportions were still generous, paneled walls rising to an open-beamed ceiling, the center of which was supported by the carved escutcheon of Ormsby. I strolled over to the huge fireplace, which I judged to be nine feet across, its carved mantel higher than my head. An extremely large log blazed upon the irons for this warm July evening, and I stepped back from the blast of heat.

"Come, my lord," Caroline called playfully. "Surely you are not cold on such an evening as this." She waved me onward and indicated the chair to her left. "We always keep the room heated to prevent the tapestries from mildewing, m'lord. I'm sure the practice is the same in your own house." Seated at the head of the table, Caroline's crown of braided hair came alive and glowed golden in the firelight.

I directed my attention to the liveried footmen clad in

green and gold who stood behind each chair. Settling into my designated place, my heart gave an extra thump as I recognized the footman attending André to be one of the roughly clad troops so newly arrived at Tregenna.

Seated across from me, the Frenchman lay back in his chair relaxed and sleepy eyed, his fingers lightly curled around a burnished goblet.

As Caroline leaned forward to take up her cup, my eye caught the rounded swells of her breast thrust against the low neckline of her dress and I thought; Minx! She knows what her body does to me and she flaunts it! She taunts me when I am helpless. Oh, at that moment how I longed to get my hands on her, and not only her beautiful neck!

The man André stirred himself sufficiently to command the footman at my back. "Fill my Lord Pettigrew's goblet, man. Do not let his cup go empty!"

The Frenchman lifted his cup and proposed a toast: "Caroline—and Pettigrew—long life and fruitful bounty to you and Good Queen Bess who governs all our lives."

With an irritated frown, Caroline returned the untouched goblet to the table, refusing to honor the toast. "Methinks you are too eager to see me married, André," she snapped, "with little concern for the outcome."

"*Au contraire,* my dear one, I am content that all will be well," he assured her suavely, and with an artless little shrug, he innocently regarded Caroline over the rim of his cup.

The very glibness of his response made me uncomfortable. I could not believe that any man who loved Caroline would willingly release her to another. Warily I scanned his carefree, oblivious visage and found no malice there. Unless . . . unless he knew with certainty that there was no possibility of my ever claiming my intended bride.

I found Caroline's intense gaze upon my face. Our glances locked and I read fear and warning in her eyes. My dear Caroline, how I loved you that moment. Intrigue and danger swirled around us and all I could think of was holding you in my arms. I drew in a deep breath and focused my attention on the slice of venison on my plate, though I had no appetite.

As I concentrated upon a mouthful of meat, I looked

up to find myself the cynosure of all eyes. In mid-bite I halted, listening; as the others, already alerted, were intently engaged. Through the high mullioned window came the sound of an approaching entourage. Hoofbeats clattered below, muffled voices called out and were answered, a dog barked and yelped into silence.

André's knife and fork, poised over his plate, resumed their sawing as he darted a guarded look at our hostess. "Ah, Caroline, it seems that your uncle has appeared in time to sup with us after all. Velasco, move your plate to the side and allow his lordship to gain his rightful place at the head of the table."

The small dark man complied without question. Nodding his head and standing, he allowed the footman to bring up another chair and then move his plate and table setting next to André.

I wondered at Velasco's docile obedience. So far this evening he had initiated no conversation, content to sit quietly hunched at the table, head bowed, attending well our remarks but responding only in monosyllables when addressed. Unlike Caroline, André and myself, who plunged directly into the meal set before us, he'd mouthed a brief, silent prayer before partaking. Thereafter he'd kept his eyes lowered to his food. Just what role did this odd little man play in this household?

In minutes Lord Ormsby strode boldly into the chamber, bringing with him a breath of chill air and the faint odor of leather and animal expected of a man who spent the day in a saddle. Caroline ran to his side and he bent his gray head to kiss her forehead, bestowing upon her a wide, affectionate smile. My Lord Ormsby was a barrel-chested man of perhaps fifty years, with smooth ruddy cheeks and a hawkish nose. He surveyed the table with shrewd glance. "Ah, Lord Pettigrew, I presume," he said, holding out his hand to me. "Welcome to Tregenna. I regret my absence when the queen's message arrived or I would have been present to greet you. I knew your father well and admired him."

We'd all risen at his entrance and he now signaled for us to be seated.

"Forgive me, Caroline, for not washing away the stains of the road, but I hoped you'd be tolerant under the circumstances since I have been eager to meet your affianced." He beamed at me as a lackey set a plate in front of him, and he began to eat with hearty gusto while directing questions to Caroline and the two men.

Ormsby's effusion at first puzzled me and then began to make me suspicious. Replete at last, he waved for more wine to be passed around the table and, leaning back in his chair, folded his hands over his rounded belly. "What news of court, Pettigrew?" he demanded jovially. "Does Elizabeth still dote upon that pretty boy, Essex? And what of Scotland's James? Does he yet sputter on behalf of his mother Mary's claim to the throne?"

We chatted amiably, touching upon the gossip and rumors rife among the royal circle, although it required no superior faculty of observation to note that both André and Caroline fidgeted in their chairs, with other matters upon their respective minds. Their exchanged glances flew across the table like a flock of homing pigeons deprived of a coop. Had the situation been of less critical proportions I might well have found myself enjoying the intrigue. Velasco, his hands folded primly at the table's edge, kept his head lowered, but his watchful eyes shifted back and forth, missing nothing.

No longer able to contain his impatience, André broke into the conversation with a casually formed question: "I hope, Sir Peter, that your trip was a fruitful one and that we may now begin the expansion program for the estate as we planned?" Tilting back his cup, Lord Ormsby drained off the last drops of wine and, smacking his lips, allowed the younger man to wait for an answer. "Quite so, André," he said at last. "And by your question, may I assume that you've recruited additional workers to clear the land and build the new mill?"

"They arrived at twilight, m'lord, and await your instructions. I'd expected you earlier and—"

Ormsby cut him off in mid-sentence, his voice deadly serious, the eyes steely cold. "I assure you, my friend, the delay was unavoidable. The Magistrate of Trewsbury hailed me upon the road and I had no choice but to stop to hear his claim. It seemed he'd unearthed a Catholic priest and his protector concealing themselves in a yeoman's barn." Ormsby's glance carefully traveled to each face waiting expectantly around the table. "The good constable requested my services in the hanging of the villainous pair."

From the end of the table I heard Caroline's gasp, and turned to see her eyes wide with shock, her pale lips parted and trembling.

André sprang to his feet, hands spread wide on the table as he leaned forward, outrage evident on his grimly set features. "My God, Ormsby," he demanded, "was there nothing you could do to prevent such a foul atrocity?"

Lord Ormsby leveled a hard look at the young Frenchman. "Prevent it, André, my friend?" he countered softly. "By God's blood, it was my duty as a true and loyal subject of Elizabeth, my queen, to see the villains dangle by their necks till the last breath was choked from their throats."

Sickened, Caroline turned away from her uncle, covering her eyes with an unsteady hand.

Velasco said nothing, but horror registered upon his face as though the grisly scene had been enacted before his eyes.

Ormsby calmly returned André's angry stare. For a breathless moment the pair remained locked in a wordless duel. Then a long, painful sigh escaped from the younger man's lips, and drawing back, he sank into his chair. He leaned his head against the red damask cushion, and closed his eyes as though exhausted. His throat worked convulsively and I saw a small vein throbbing at his pale temple.

A faint, complacent smile curved Ormsby's mouth as he turned his regard to me. "I'm sure that *you* will agree with me as a law-abiding citizen, Lord Pettigrew, that though the measures are drastic, it's the only way to deal with these seditious papists who invade our country and undermine the loyalty of its citizens."

Before answering, I gazed around the table, pausing to observe the disquiet his remarks had produced on the other members of the household. Lord Ormsby appeared untouched by their distress. Curiously I found myself speculating at my host's sangfroid. When all those around him reacted with abhorrence to a cruel punishment, he alone chose to see its validity. Perhaps until this moment I'd not fully appreciated the man's enormous villainy. For now, it served no purpose to cross verbal swords with him.

"Indeed, my lord," I agreed reluctantly. "The law of the land doth quote all priests to be traitors and those who succor them, guilty of a felonious act. But consider also, when Pope Gregory excommunicated Elizabeth from the Church, not only did he declare her to be a heretic to be deprived of dominion and title, but also absolved those who would murder her as guiltless of sin." I rested my folded arms on the table and stared down into my empty plate. "Truly, one may feel compassion for the guiltless cleric intent only upon the salvation of his flock. But as the pendulum retraces its swing, so do we find the rabid theologian bent upon the murderous overthrow of Elizabeth, secure in the apostolic blessing that his act will win him a shining throne in heaven."

The Frenchman's chair scraped against the flagstones, a raucous screech shattering the tense quiet. Recovered from his earlier outburst, he smiled wryly, a flicker of humor lighting his eyes. "Methinks, Lord Pettigrew, that for a Protestant thou dost display an amazing flexibility of mind. Perhaps more so than I would have expected from one hand-picked by a worried queen." Turning his head to the drooping Caroline, he grinned. "I believe, Caroline, 'my love,' that I shall favor your union with my blessing. We may find in your betrothed the material of a convert."

André's remark aroused Caroline from her dull-eyed depression, for she immediately sat up and glared at the young man beside her. "I'll thank you *not* to pass me between you like a platter of cold mutton." She inclined her bright head sharply in my direction. "Pettigrew already knows that I will have none of him. Do you understand, André?" Folding her arms defiantly across her chest, her seething eyes flashed at her uncle and she skewered him with her keen gaze. "Have I made myself quite clear, Uncle?"

In the benign fashion that I mistrusted, Ormsby chuckled and, pushing himself away from the table, stretched his arms wearily over his head. "I am much too tired to debate this matter tonight, my dear. We shall pursue it further tomorrow. But since our guest has made such a long journey to benefit his suit," he suggested reasonably, "I think it only proper that we make an effort to entertain him. André and I are unfortunately engaged with estate business tomorrow, but surely I may count upon your generosity to have some pity on the man. Guide him upon a tour of Tregenna lands as they are known only by you, my dear. Dine al fresco under the leaning willows and we shall resume the discussion next evening. For now, good night, Caroline, André, dear Velasco. I yearn for my bed."

Caroline's mouth came open to argue but then snapped shut in resignation. Her uncle had already turned from her on his way out. She sighed dispiritedly, lifting her shoulders in a shrug of defeat, and redirected her attention to me. "Well, my lord, it appears free choice is no longer my option to exercise. I shall send my servant to collect you when you have breakfasted. And now, if you'll excuse me, I wish to have a private word with André."

Thus dismissed, I made my bows to my hostess and the other two gentlemen and withdrew. As I last glimpsed him, Velasco stood staring into the waning flames within the huge hearth, his head bent, his hands clasped as though in prayer.

Good nature restored to him, André bid me a smiling good night, and as the door closed I saw his arm encircle Caroline's shoulder.

Chapter 11

I considered listening at the door, but as I hesitated a footman crossed the foyer, and better judgment sent me up the staircase and down the darkened hall to my quarters. What I'd seen and heard this night puzzled me and I knew not what course to follow. No one was as he seemed. But for that matter, neither was I. One thing was certain, however, Lord Ormsby definitely wanted me away from the castle tomorrow. Caroline was to be his instrument in this distraction, and I was not adverse to letting her distract me. One could not, I reasoned, be dutiful the full sweep of the clock. Besides, I'd already promised myself another cautious trip downstairs when the house grew silent and the others had found their beds.

The tension in the dining room this evening had bordered upon hysteria. The players had remained superficially serene but I'd sensed a strong undercurrent of fear, invisible yet real as a coiled snake. Its presence had permeated the atmosphere and I intended to focus my nocturnal investigation upon the stage where this strong emotion had played its course.

As I entered my room, instinct or a sixth sense, call it what you will, warned me that an intruder had recently been there. No doubt one of Ormsby's agents had searched my belongings. A bench stood not quite as squared as I left it. A traveling case, too, leaned slightly askew from the place where it had been set. I smiled smugly to myself. A private search had been expected and I knew it had revealed nothing. In that respect I had nothing to fear. Fully dressed, I stretched out on my bed, my hands behind my head. The fatigue of the day closed in, crowding jumbled thoughts and visions of Caroline. I slept.

Perhaps three hours later, I awoke to a dark, silent house. Again instinct served me and I rose on one elbow, ears alert. Had there been a muffled clatter in the court below? Possibly departing hoof beats sounding smothered in the early hours? I swung my legs over the side of the high bed and stood blinking away the sleep that fogged my senses. When I had fully awakened by the light of the guttering candle at the bedside, I moved to the door. I expected to be watched but counted on the hour to dull the perception of my keeper. Silently I turned the knob, and content that no eyes watched, I slipped into the corridor. My eyes soon adjusted to the darkness and I made my way, agile as a shadow, down the steps of the central staircase. A footman, chin on chest, dozed on a bench in a narrow alcove, but reassured by the loud rumbles and snorts issuing from his nose and mouth, I edged across the foyer and into the dining chamber I'd vacated mere hours ago. Leaning against the closed door, I listened fearfully to the loud rasp of my own breathing. Gradually my heart's wild thumping quieted and I made a slow, careful survey of the room. Through the great, high window with its leaded red and blue glass escutcheon came a glimmer of light from an outside torch. In the hearth the red embers of a dying fire still glowed. Drawn to it, I stared down into the smoking coals and recalled Velasco standing in the same place, head bowed, a supplicant's attitude in every line of the slight, tense body. Gazing down at the smoldering ruins of the huge oak log, I became aware of footprints among the ashes that had not been there earlier. They led outward from within the fireplace's huge blackened cavity, appearing to emerge from a substantial side wall at the left of the opening.

I clapped myself on the side of the head, appalled by my own density. Of course! A priest hole! This evening while Ormsby, the others and I discussed the precarious fate of the illicit priesthood, one or more of the poor, beleaguered lot crouched in the hiding place, scant feet away, sweating out an unenviable fate. I understood now why such a formidable log burned industriously on a warm July evening. I was relieved that the poor beggar had galloped on his way and I had not been the instrument of his capture.

I stepped into the darkened niche, my fingertips probing a wall seam where I suspected a concealed entry existed. Immediately the pressure of my searching hands sent a partition retracting into the wall, revealing the black oblong entrance to a hidden compartment.

From a silver candelabra in the main room I extracted a candle and, lighting it with a hot coal, held it aloft; a hideaway built skillfully into the fireplace, I marveled. Most clever. The "green men," as they were called, those who constructed such seditious places, obviously designed their work with great cunning. A narrow cot and a rickety table comprised the simple furnishings. Next to a spent, sooty candle gleamed a small brass crucifix. There came again the depressing sense of those who'd so recently inhabited these surroundings. Their terror still infused the air, the stench of fear vile in my nostrils. Disturbed, eager to set my mind to other matters, I backed out of the tiny sanctuary.

The shadowy chamber, used as an informal dining hall by the immediate family, also served as a trophy room. Articles of the hunt, swords and shields, mounted heads of deer, boar and wildcats decorated the paneled walls. Skirting the long table I raised the candle to better see the hanging paraphernalia and then, remembering the danger of the unsheltered light, lowered it to a nearby sideboard. As I did so I caught sight of a ghastly creature, coiled and scaly, rearing its head to strike. My heart leaped, shrieking in my chest! Instinctively I sprang back, my hand on the dagger at my waist, and then froze, blinking in amazement. The frightful apparition remained poised, unmoving, in a state of suspended animation. I gaped and felt hot blood coursing in my cheeks. I'd nearly fought off the attack of a stuffed snake, a loathsome souvenir of some past hunt. Still feeling foolish, I willed my heart to a saner pace just as a voice at my shoulder again sent that laboring organ pounding in my chest.

"There are enough two-legged reptiles in this viper's nest to warrant yer attention, m'lord, wi'out plaguin' the poor dead ones." Cedric's dry chuckle tickled my ear.

And then his hard fingers fastened on my arm, warning me to silence. He cast a wary glance over his shoulder and urged me toward the wall. "Quickly, m'lord, get thee behind the tapestry. I be sure I heard voices just outside the door."

As the door swung open, we just managed to slip into the scant foot of space between the wall and the huge wall covering. As we hastened to shelter I'd snuffed the candle in the palm of my hand, fearing its smoke would be detected. I winced now, fingering the blistered flesh. Once the new arrivals lighted candles I was surprised to find I could easily see and identify them. It appeared Lord Ormsby made a habit of spying on conversations. The Flanders tapestry had been woven in such a manner that there was a horizontal opening undetectable from the reverse side which provided a clear view of the entire room. Cedric and I flattened ourselves against the cold stone wall and remained motionless.

Twenty feet away Lord Ormsby focused his full attention on pouring wine into a goblet. At the refectory table, Caroline was equally engrossed with the task of lighting tapers in silver holders. Her loosened hair lay upon the proud slope of her shoulders and flowed down her back. She'd replaced the purple gown she'd worn to supper with a simple azure blue robe. My breath caught in my throat as she lifted her eyes and her gaze, direct and piercing, seemed to bore straight through me. But as she gave no sign of being aware of me, I allowed the air to slowly ease out of my taut lungs.

Ormsby sipped pensively at the wine, regarding his niece over the rim of the cup with eyes as bright and evil as those of the stuffed snake I'd encountered earlier. Caroline seated herself at the table and folded her hands solemnly in her lap, her accusing eyes fixed on her uncle. He shifted uncomfortably in his chair, attempting to avoid the girl's merciless scrutiny.

"Has André set out with Philip and Father Jacob?" he asked finally.

"Yes, Uncle," Caroline replied in a cold voice, her stare raking his flushed face.

Ormsby studied the contents of his cup, swirling the wine absently. He pursed his lips as though thinking how to frame his next words. "You're still upset, I presume, because of my actions at Trewsbury?" he said, avoiding her eyes.

Caroline jumped to her feet, her hand shaking in a barely controlled rage. "Angry!" she cried. "I'm horrified. How could you have done such a monstrous thing, Uncle? Father Jonathan and Toren Biddle were our friends and you betrayed them! How in God's eyes can you justify such action?"

Ormsby quickly glanced at the door. "Calm yourself, Caroline," he hissed in a steely voice. "This is not the time for hysterics, girl. In the name of reason keep your voice down. There are strangers in the house who are close to Elizabeth!"

"Damn Pettigrew!" she yelled, ignoring his warning. "Why shouldn't I be hysterical? I've been out of my mind for the past ten months. It is only now that my eyes have been opened and I begin to see you for what you are."

Ormsby slammed his cup down on the table. "In God's name, woman!" he spat through clenched teeth, "can't you see that I had no choice? The priest and Toren understood. Why can't you? To do anything else would have cast suspicion on me as well as the activities at Tregenna. Get that into your sentimental head! A few moments' bravado could have destroyed the planning of months!"

Caroline whirled away from her uncle, emitting a strangled exclamation of disgust. Folding her arms across her chest she fought to control the revulsion trembling on her lips. When she spoke the irony in her tone cut the air with its bitterness. "When you originally involved me in this plot, Uncle, I believed all your glib lies. How could I not? You were the only family I'd ever known. Surely *you* would not use me and my fortune to serve some vile conspiracy." Caroline brought her hands together, bowing her head over the tightly entwined fingers. "We were to smuggle priests into England to serve the needs of starving Catholic souls deprived of guidance, you told me. Surely this was part of God's holy work, I told myself. But it's become less than holy, has it not, Uncle? It is no longer simple men of God that we've been guiding into the interior, is it? What we've nurtured, and what I so foolishly thought such a noble cause, has nefariously become an *unholy* network of spies! Agents of France and Spain who would assassinate the queen and bring foreign rule to Englishmen!" Caroline swung around to face her uncle. "You've sold your country for a pile of gold pieces, I'll wager, Uncle, but I'll not stay to aid your chicanery further. I deceived myself into trusting you, believing you innocent of the evil your acts have caused, but today when you assisted in the murder of two honest men to preserve your . . . iniquity, that was the final straw!" Caroline broke off breathlessly, her eyes dark circles of condemnation.

Ormsby sat unmoving while Caroline denounced him, his head sunk on his chest, his expression masked. The slits of his eyes gleamed red in the candlelight. "Exactly what do you plan to do?" he asked in a dead voice.

Caroline shook her head in confusion, one hand covering her forehead. "I—I already told you. I must leave this place." She straightened, dropping her hand. "But before I go, you must promise me to cease this illicit contraband of humans." The sherry eyes glittered with their promised threat. "Because I warn you, if you do not, I shall expose you; even—even if I must forfeit my own life, I will see that you are stopped!"

Even in the warm glow of the candlelight, Ormsby's face grayed and seemed to grow old. Before my eyes a strong, virile man shriveled. With an anguished groan he held out his arms, speaking Caroline's name in supplication.

"Oh, my dear child, my dear little Caroline," he babbled, his head shaking as though palsied. "Of course you are right! You are right to condemn me but I was so *afraid*. I did not intend that matters should go to *these* lengths." His frightened eyes widened with a look of helplessness. "I meant only to succor my fellow believers, but the Duke de Guise allowed me no quarter. He would have my throat slit as easily as he would order a fowl's neck rung." A large, shining tear trembled on Ormsby's lower lash and quivered there, then tumbled down his ruddy cheek.

Caroline stared, unsure but wanting to believe her uncle. Then, with a forgiving cry, she rushed into his embrace.

"*Dear* Uncle," she murmured against his shoulder. "I knew you could not willingly commit such crimes. Forgive me if I've hurt you; I did not know what to think. Surely you must understand?"

Beside me Cedric silently grimaced in disbelief, echoing my own sentiments. Ormsby's change of face was a little *too* sudden to be credible. I feared that Caroline in her emotional state was particularly vulnerable to her uncle's clever acting. She was more than a little naive, and left herself open to destruction if Ormsby was *not* sincere. If he'd told me the sun shone on a perfect day I would be inclined to seek shelter from the storm.

Caroline drew away from her uncle's arms, sniffing and wiping away the tears with the back of her hand. "I still mean to go," she said, her voice resolute and firm. "I can no longer remain knowing what evil has transpired inside these walls. Tomorrow I shall ride to London with André and the man Pettigrew. Perhaps if I speak to the queen personally, she will relieve me of the commitment of this absurd marriage. But have no fear, Uncle; no hint of your intrigue shall pass my lips."

Ormsby, too, made a show of mopping his face and clearing his throat, pleading: "Do not go so soon, my dear little Caroline. Stay with me one more week, I beg of you. I must disperse the men and receive Sir Amyiot and Wilkens, who are en route from Reims. I've already been paid for their passage and I dare not defy the Duke de Guise. Amyiot is his personal agent and if something should befall him, my life would be forfeited."

Caroline stood for a moment, head bowed, eyes focused upon her clasped hands. "Very well, Uncle, I shall remain. But when the seventh day fades to twilight, I shall be gone. Come with us or stay, whichever brings you peace. Whatever your course, I shall pray for you, for you shall very well need all the help God may grant."

Lord Ormsby took a tentative step forward and gazed down into Caroline's implacable face. I could only guess at the cost of her superficial coldness. She bled within, suffering beneath her masquerade of hardness, suffering the need for it. Ormsby's hooded eyes dwelled on the curve of Caroline's gleaming head. He opened his lips to speak, but then, divining Caroline's resolution, said nothing and turning, he went to the door. When it closed after him, Caroline sighed heavily, her eyes closing on her internal grief. At last she stirred, and as though burdened with a thousand sorrows, followed him out of the room.

More than ever I wished I could give her sanctuary in my arms. My inner self cried out to shelter her and to offer a warm shoulder upon which she might shed her silent tears.

Cedric's elbow found my rib cage. "We'd better be gettin' to bed, m'lord, before we 'ave another bloody confrontation on our 'ands."

I grunted my assent and he and I slipped out from behind the tapestry, but not before Cedric stopped to run his hands over the stonework that had been directly at his back. "Hmm . . ." He compressed his lips thoughtfully as his fingers inquisitively played upon the rough seams between the stones. With a triumphant "Ahhh," he put his shoulder to a likely section of the wall and it swung inward upon silent hinges. We both peered into the black void. I started forward but seeing nothing, pulled back. Cedric reluctantly followed suit. "Just as I thought," he muttered jubilantly to himself. "The whole place is honeycombed wi' these secret passages, I'll warrant, m'lord." The faded blue eyes glowed in anticipation. "If ya 'ave no need o' my services tomorrow, m'lord, I be thinkin' I might do a leetle explorin' behind the scenes. A sneakin' feelin' in these old bones tells me we may just need another exit from this place. Mark my words, lad."

Chapter 12

True to her word, Caroline sent a servant to guide me to the stables the following morning. I found my lady impatiently waiting, already mounted on a frisky gray mare who tossed its silken black mane and side-stepped skittishly as I approached. Zortan, my own steed, great-spirited black beast that he was, eyed the mare and its rider with a sort of superior disdain and snuffled a damp greeting against my cheek. Laughing, I pulled my-self up into the saddle and greeted my restive hostess.

She sat confidently on her mount, apparently at ease in the awkward Spanish sidesaddle, the sweep of her burgundy skirts richly contrasting with the animal's glinting silver coat. A low-crowned beaver rested on Caroline's golden braids, its nonsensical red plume curled audaciously beneath her ear. "And a pleasant good morning to you, my Lord Pettigrew," she responded, casting a dubious look skyward. "Although methinks the bright beginnings of this day may well dissolve into a thundering deluge." She nodded westward and I turned in the saddle toward the direction she indicated. Black thunderheads crowded upon the horizon, a dark smudge upon an otherwise flawless day.

I drew the sweet morning air into my lungs, not willing to forfeit this opportunity to be alone with Caroline. I shrugged away the possibility of rain. "We shall be snug within Tregenna again before that bit of mist may do us any damage, my lady. Trust my weatherman's eye and we shall still have a pleasant day to browse among the wonders of Tregenna—as only you know them, to quote your uncle." I cocked an eye toward the baskets that straddled the mare's withers. "And . . . to dine al fresco beneath the willows," I added smugly.

Caroline brushed her riding crop lightly across the mare's rump and horse and rider took off at a trot, streaking out of the courtyard in a shower of pebbles. "Come along, Pettigrew," she called over her shoulder. "See if that bowlegged nag of yours can catch my Valkyrie!"

"Call me names if you must, Caroline," I shouted after her. "But dare not insult my horse!" I roused Zortan with a kick, and we galloped in pursuit.

We pounded happily across the grassy slopes of the deer park, elms and beeches and dark green pines spreading their dappled shade upon the ground. For a quarter of a mile I held Zortan in check, thundering at Caroline's heels. He, chafing at his bit, resisted my rein, not content to be second to a female's hack, nor was he to be daunted by the lighthearted feather in the lady's hat.

Caroline triumphantly drew to a halt at a rocky outcropping of land where yellow lichen webbed smooth, ancient stone. The mare threw back her head, blowing through quivering nostrils, nickering jubilantly. Between my knees Zortan trembled with sullen indignation as we came abreast of Caroline.

"Poor Zortan," she commiserated, pouting in sympathy. "Your mouth must be prodigiously sore from your master's misguided chivalry." Her eyes dancing with mischief, Caroline directed her gaze at me as she leaned sideways to scratch the stallion's forehead. "You are bursting to show me your heels while Pettigrew here strains his muscles to frustrate you." Caroline's chin came up pugnaciously. "Is that the way you would handle a spirited wife, m'lord? Bridled and checked until she bowed to your wish?"

I leaned back in the saddle, resting my hands upon the pommel. "Well, that *is* indeed progress, Zortan," I addressed the horse. "Last night she would have no part of me, and in truth consigned me to perdition, and yet she now coyly inquires into my habits as a spouse. Do you think, perhaps, there is hope for my suit after all?" I tried not to laugh at Caroline's burst of sputtering rage. "Pettigrew—" she said threateningly, her voice grating. "Pettigrew—you—you—" She sucked in a lungful of air, ready to discharge it in a graphic tirade. Closing her eyes, she clamped her lips tightly together. Then, teetering a moment on indecision, the corners of her mouth twitched and drew back in a conceding grin. "Pettigrew, you fool." She chuckled. "Meet your equal. We are two fools and it's proper that we talk to horses. For they among us are the only ones with sense." She held out her hand, the amber eyes warm upon my face. "Pax, my lord?" she questioned softly.

I closed my fingers over hers. "Aye, lady. Pax it is and a mellow peace—for now—until the next time."

"Damn you, Pettigrew," she agreed cheerfully. "You are right. There can never be peace between us. Rage and fury, passion and grief, but never peace." A sadness crept across her face, dimming her exuberance. "It's the peaks and valleys for us, m'lord. The heights and depths, but never a quiet harbor, I fear."

The same dark forboding chilled me with its presence but I would not be intimidated. "Not so, Lady Caroline. The voice of doom whispering in your ear is merely Zeus rattling his thunderbolts. See? It is as you predicted, I regret to say. We shall have a storm upon us in an hour or so." I pointed toward the shore. Huge, jostling clouds, swollen and black, advanced across the gray sea. Zortan and Valkyrie sniffed the air, nostrils aquiver, and fretted uneasily beneath us. "Would you return to the castle, my lady?"

Caroline tilted her head back slightly, a smiling challenge upon her red lips, the arrogant feather aflutter against her soft cheek. "How little you know of me, m'lord," she charged softly. "But let this be your first lesson. I *never* go back. My course is always forward, whatever the consequences. Once I've trod a path, then it is as gone and dead as yesterday." At her whim, the mood shifted. "Besides, Pettigrew," she asserted brightly, tapping the basket before her, "I've prepared a prodigious feast and I refuse to allow it to go unappreciated. Meat and cheese and rosy apples, wine to warm your blood and honey cake to sweeten your disposition. What say you to that?"

Caroline's gay insolence scattered the shadows like chaff upon the wind, and I refused to allow doubt or suspicion to spoil this precious time between us. For the moment I shut my mind to the conversation that Cedric and I had overheard the night before. No intrigue brewed at Tregenna. I was a simple Englishman returned from foreign travels, free of political responsibilities, eager to know and love this exasperating, complex, adorable woman by my side. In answer to her question I retorted, "Why—I say, then, forward, my lady, since that is the only course open to us." I nudged Zortan with my heels. "Let us begone, horse! Chivalry is dead and we shall show the wench who is her master!" At a gallop Zortan tore down the gorse-covered incline toward the breathless sea. Caroline's shrieks were caught by and scattered in the wind. "We'll see who's master," she squealed, laughing. "We'll . . . see . . ."

Caroline and I passed the ensuing hours in what seemed a timeless void. A shallow track brought us to the beach. We trotted along its fringe, blithely engrossed with one another. Foaming surf swirled and tumbled about the nimble hooves of the animals. The air breathed the storm's warning but its dirge was but a nymph's sweet song to my enchanted ears. Wandering aimlessly, we trailed crisscrossing paths through the wet sand, oblivious to the rising tide that swarmed upon those steps and blurred away our passing. I looked back once, but Caroline's hand upon my sleeve would allow my thoughts no further digression. And looking down into her face, I needed no other diversion. From the sandy shelf we ascended a natural stone staircase to the cliffs above. As we crested the promontory, a single stroke of lightning stabbed at a wind-gnarled pine. The blackened bark sizzled and flamed, and immediately the sky discharged its watery load upon us.

Heads bent low, we galloped over the soggy turf. This time I followed Caroline's lead and we sprinted full tilt into the meager sanctuary of a huge sheltering oak. Sharply reined in, Valkyrie reared back on her hind legs, muddied hooves flailing. Controlling the frightened animal, Caroline raised her voice over the crashing din. "We can't stay here!" she shouted. "The storm will last for hours. There's an old mill near here . . ."

She waved me forward and again we raced across a sodden field trammeled by the pouring rain. Slowing our frantic pace, we turned into a narrow path that slanted roughly upward. Trees and brush crowding closely overhead formed a darkened canopy that deflected the gray mass of falling water. Still it rattled loudly in our ears and the rutted lane rapidly dissolved into a river of red mud. We broke into an overgrown clearing and I spied the silent waterwheel of an ancient mill. Tenacious vines encroached upon the sagging structure, weighing it down, nearly consumming it. Caroline bounded for a shed immediately adjacent, which I guessed to be a barn of sorts. A door hung listlessly open and we raced toward it, ducking our heads to gain entry. Surprisingly the roof was sound and the four of us, riders and horses, stamped to a halt, startled to find ourselves within dry cover. I swung down quickly and raised my arms to Caroline, who promptly offered me the picnic basket. She slid from the saddle on her own, wet to the skin, the proud red feather lank upon her cheek. "This is not the willowy glen my uncle offered you last night, my lord, but under the circumstances I hope it meets with your approval."

I gave the small stable a thoughtful inspection. "Its snug dryness commends it to me, my lady, but had I a choice in the matter, perhaps a small fireplace would have taken precedence over this imaginative decor." I raised my eyes significantly to the festoons of cobwebs draped upon the low rafters.

"Well, my lord," she humored me, "if the mere presence of a hearth will bring sunshine into your otherwise dismal day, then follow me." Through a low door we gained access into the larger chamber of the mill itself. Stairs led upward, and from the sound of the rain I surmised that a portion of the roof lay open to the weather. Where we stood, however, was dry and free of drafts and miraculously, housed a small stone fireplace. A pile of logs was neatly stacked beside it, and fresh straw, conveniently scattered, lay heaped against the near partition. It occurred to me that we were expected.

Caroline noticed my cynical smirk. "If you think that I've lured you here with devious intent, my lord, may I say that often the local shepherds use this place as shelter from just such weather. I've seen them myself and presume it is they who have provided the stump of a candle and the dry blankets draped upon the bench." The lie rolled glibly from her tongue. I did not believe her tale of weather-bound herders. But the thought did pounce upon my reason that the abandoned old mill might be an excellent hideaway for a smuggled priest, should the castle be under surveillance.

I contrived a bland smile. "Frankly, my Lady Caroline, I care not for the source of this unexpected good fortune, only that it satisfy my needs." I heard a muffled whinny from the outer room. "But first I must attend the horses." I set the luncheon basket deliberately at her feet and retired to the stable to wipe down the shivering horses with fists full of dry hay.

When I returned a welcoming fire leapt upon the hearth and our repast lay spread upon a linen cloth over the straw. A sumptuous platter of sliced beef stirred the saliva under my tongue and the sight of yellow cheese and golden bread awakened my dormant appetite.

Caroline poured red wine from an earthen jug into silver cups and held one out to me. "This will warm the inside of you, Pettigrew, if not the out." Abruptly she set down the cups and, turning away, gave a large, wet sneeze.

"God's blessings upon you Caroline," I said. "Methinks you had best get out of those drenched vestments lest the ague befall you and inflame your lungs."

Caroline looked down at the outcropping of her chest. "I can vouch for the soundness of my lungs, m'lord," she retorted dryly, "and will not bare them to prove it." She tried to gulp back another sneeze but it would not be denied. The forceful snap of her head sent her bedraggled hat into the middle of our intended meal. She stared round eyed at the fallen headpiece, and picking it up with thumb and forefinger, disdainfully flung it into a corner. "Very well, my lord," she said reasonably. "I shall remove *my* clothes on the condition that you as well remove *yours.*" The gleam in the amber eyes told me she thought to call my bluff.

Little did she know me. I stood up and began removing my wet doublet.

The gleam faded.

After the doublet I peeled off the waistcoat and shirt, dropping them in a pile on the straw. Divesting myself of sword and dagger, I reached for my belt.

With an embarrassed squeal, Caroline turned her back to me. "Damn you, Pettigrew," she snapped, her cheeks flaming. "Why must you be so stubborn?"

I widened my eyes at her rigid back. *"I,* stubborn?" I repeated incredulously.

For a second she fumed, digesting my last comment, and then, reaching over to the bench, flung a blanket at my head. "Oh, very well," she said grudgingly. "I shall remove my clothes, but while I am about it, pray occupy your devouring eyes *elsewhere!"*

Swallowing a chuckle, I wrapped the blanket around my shoulders and squatted down to consider the succulent meal at my feet.

Shortly Caroline's bare feet, extending from beneath a blanket which she clutched under her chin, appeared within my line of vision. I looked up the length of her and met the contained fury in her face.

Pouring wine into a silver cup, I held it out to her. "This will soothe your jangled nerves, my lady."

She accepted with ill grace and sank down into the straw, eying me suspiciously. "Do *not* think, my lord, that because I have been reduced to such a compromising state that I can be . . . easily compromised," she advised peremptorily. "We are but fellow voyagers victimized by the same circumstances."

"Of course, my lady." I reached for the dagger and began sawing upon the loaf of bread. "Perhaps some food will settle your groundless fears."

I continued to fill the lady's cup each time its shining bottom reappeared as we dined in noble abundance. When she was at last replete, Caroline licked her fingers with little smacking sounds, slapping her hand over her mouth as she emitted a vigorous hiccough. She tightened the blanket more securely around her person. "I just want you to know, my good Lord Pettigrew," she informed me owlishly, obviously having some difficulty in focusing, "that I am a noble and sedate lady—and I am no man's winch." Outrageously tipsy, she giggled.

"I mean wench," she corrected drowsily, and slowly sank sideways and into my waiting arms.

Time seemed to stop as she slept curled against my side. She'd unbound the vibrant gold hair from its confining braids and it spread in loving tendrils about her shoulders. Like tentacles they drew and held me as I, a willing prisoner, sat quietly, content to provide warmth and protection for my lady as she dreamed.

Chapter 13

The rain continued its harsh barrage against the roof, but held no threat. Dancing flames on the hearth gradually grew subdued and quietly licked at the crumbling logs as Caroline stirred in my arms. As the dark-fringed eyes slowly opened, my impatient yearnings quickened and I brushed her parted lips with my own.

She started awake but then, with an instinctive whimper of desire, entwined her arms around my neck. Her eager kiss sent a joyous elation coursing through my body.

She drew back silently, her eyes wide and questioning, and then I felt her warm breath, and the tip of her tongue lay a gentle path upon my lower lip. She tasted my flesh tentatively and then set her teeth lightly to its soft moistness, her mouth kneading and sucking until desire pounded in my blood. She did not struggle as I stripped away the blanket covering her body, but merely lay back in my arms, the amber eyes expectant and unafraid. She'd crossed her slender white arms over her breasts and I drew her hands away, placing a lingering kiss in the palm of each. Lowering my head I touched my lips to one proud, flushed nipple. She shuddered, flinching, but tightening my hold I pressed her closer. "A bird does not fly on one wing alone, my dear," I murmured, and set my mouth to the other trembling breast.

Feverishly Caroline's arms tightened around my neck. My hands smoothed downward over the slimness of her young body, circling the narrow waist, moving to cup the rounded hips, pressing them intimately, urgently closer. Lightning exploded overhead and the rain, lashing and insistent, sent its torrents down on the old mill. But already we'd shut out the world and its elements. Nothing existed beyond the four walls that sheltered us. All I desired I held in my arms.

I awoke in darkness. Water dripped from invisible eaves into unseen pools like the relentless strokes of a clock ticking away the hours. Raising my head, I peered sleepily into the crumbling coals across the room, all that remained of the once blazing fire. Caroline sighed in her sleep, nuzzling my shoulder with her chin. Gradually she awoke, the flat of her hand warm against my chest, the idle fingers plucking at the black hairs growing there.

"I suppose I must marry you now, Pettigrew," she conceded dreamily. "Since you've bespoiled my maidenhood, I can see no other choice."

"Oh, indeed, my lady?" I challenged mildly. "And do *I* no longer have any say in this matter? From the time I first set foot in Tregenna you have insulted and repulsed my suit. Perhaps at last I find myself convinced that you are not suitable to stand by my side as my wife and the mother of my children."

"You lie, Pettigrew." She grinned knowingly. "For we are already committed to one another more irrevocably than had we been legally joined by all the cardinals in London." Caroline rose up on her knees and sat back on her heels. She looked down, spreading her hands over her flat belly. "Besides which, my lord, I believe that you have thoroughly impregnated me, and should you deny our relationship I shall follow you all over the land with my great swollen belly and denounce your complicity—ha!" she dared. "And what do you say to that, my lord?"

I lay back in the straw with my hands under my head. "Well . . . I should say that first of all you are a blackmailing wench and secondly that you have an exceedingly vindictive nature, a trait which will require breaking like a fractious colt."

Considering the diagnosis, I set my mouth to one side. "Perhaps a good beating will rectify the fault."

Caroline's eyes widened with mischief and without warning she jumped astride me, gleefully tearing at the hair on my chest. "Beat *me*, will you, lord of parrots?! We shall see who—"

As irresponsible as children we tussled in the straw,

the proximity of struggling bodies striking passions as flint upon flint strikes fire. Still astraddle, she stopped abruptly, the rasp of her quickened breath just below my ear. The length of her slim white body lay quivering upon mine and as I would have thrust into her, her thighs tightened on my turgid organ, halting my entry.

"Hold, oh, please hold, my dear one," she gasped. "Linger if you are able, I beg of you. I would cling to this precious time as I would cling to life."

Silently I held her, the heat of our ardor ebbing like the tide, yet I knew it would rise again to inundate and blot out all other reality. I cupped her face with one hand and she turned to kiss the palm. Her eyes traveled over my blistered flesh and she stared at it, catching her breath. She did not look up as she spoke. "I thought that it was you last night in the dining hall," she said quietly. "When I entered I noticed the missing candle. You smothered it with your hand, did you not?"

"You knew, but did not betray me?"

She shrugged. "It would have served no purpose at the time, Pettigrew, but for now, at least, it has saved the necessity of explaining the plottings of my uncle. Are you shocked at such perfidy?"

The remnants of the fire toppled. The mention of Ormsby brought a chill foreboding to the atmosphere, and instinctively I reached for the discarded blanket to cover our nakedness. Caroline's uncle loomed real and disquieting, insinuating his evil between us, a barrier driving us apart. Her hands fluttered indecisively against my chest and then she pushed away the covering, resisting the pressure of my arm. "No . . . no . . ." she whimpered, confusedly. "I can't stay here any longer. It grows late and uncle will be worried. I—"

I caught hold of her shoulders, giving them an impatient shake. "For God's sake, Caroline, why do you persist in thinking that your uncle is just a poor, misguided pawn in an affair of treachery? I fear for your safety. By denouncing your uncle's activities you have presented yourself as a threat to him. Do you honestly believe that a man who could hang two close friends out of expediency would hesitate to kill someone who threatens his very life?"

She shook her head frantically, tears wet on her cheeks. "Don't you understand? He's my uncle. He and André are all I—" She broke off, biting back the disclosure she feared to make even to me.

Unable to help myself, I cruelly dug my fingers into her soft flesh. "Who is this André and what is he to you, Caroline?" I demanded coldly. "Tell me! Do you love him?" Again I shook her savagely, the golden hair tumbling over her face. "For if you do, my sweet, with joy in my heart and with you there to watch my deed, I shall kill him." In my rage there flashed across my mind the vision of a gray-faced Caroline hanging dead between hands that clutched her throat. My God! A cold film of perspiration suddenly bathed my body and I turned away from her horrified stare. "Forgive me, my dearest," I whispered. "I could never willingly hurt you." I felt the warmth of her hand against my chest, and I turned my head slowly to meet the dark amber eyes.

A faint, sad smile was a shadow on her lips. "I fear, my love, that we are destined to hurt one another," she said. "We feel and love too passionately to be content with half measures."

I laid two silencing fingers over her lips. "Let us not speak of pain, Caroline. We've known only joy in this place today. I would not spoil it with spoken doubts and recriminations. Come," I said, lifting her to her feet. "You are right. The sky darkens and we must return to the castle."

Chapter 14

We dressed in silence, avoiding each other's eyes. We saddled and mounted our horses, and soon Zortan and Valkyrie were picking their way along the path to Tregenna. Scudding clouds shrouded the moon but the lights of the fortress offered a homing beacon. Like mindless souls we followed, unable to resist its pull. As we neared a dark clump of brush, a lone figure darted from concealment and crouching low, ran, bent double, towards us. I'd half unsheathed my sword when I heard Cedric's muted hail. Relieved, I slid the blade into its casing and after dismounting, helped Caroline to the ground.

Cedric wordlessly motioned us to follow him into the shelter of the darkened copse. Relief was evident in his throaty voice. "I was gettin' worried, m'lord. I feared a Cornish goblin ha' eaten ya."

I clapped him on the shoulder, pleased to see him. In truth, I could really see very little of him in the dark. "What news, Cedric, and why have you chosen to meet us at this unlikely spot, pray tell?" He seemed reluctant to speak in Caroline's presence, but I urged him on.

"Waaal, m'lord, since I've occupied myself the whole day, uh, performin' the leetle task ye set fer me, I thought it best that the guards at the castle think I be wuth ye and 'er ladyship."

I could not prevent my low chuckle. "Well done, Cedric, my friend. You have all the baser instincts of a true spy."

I heard Caroline's sharp intake of breath as I uttered the last word. Standing close to her I felt the sudden rigidity of her body as it tensed and surprise choked in her throat. "What are you saying, Pettigrew?" she demanded.

"That the two of you are spies, sent here by Elizabeth to—" She started at the realization as though it were too ghastly to comprehend. Furiously she tried to shrug free of the arm I held around her shoulder, but I would not be cast off.

"Damn you, Pettigrew, you bastard!" she yelled. I pulled her resisting body against me, one hand over her mouth to silence her. I had enough problems with which to deal, without the need of fighting off Ormsby's army as well. To Cedric's dark shape I snapped, "Leave us. I would have words with Lady Caroline."

He grunted his assent and slipped away to stand sentry at the edge of the thicket.

Dropping to my knees, I pulled Caroline with me. She continued to fight valiantly but soon her efforts weakened and at last she ceased to struggle, her breasts rising and falling under my restraining arm. But I knew better than to remove my hand from her mouth. Although she was exhausted, her mind was still fixed on escape. I bent my head to her ear. Kissing the lobe, I ran the tip of my tongue over its edge. "I love you, Caroline," I murmured softly so as not to be heard by Cedric. "Above all things, remember that I love you. Do you hear me? This afternoon we pledged ourselves to each other. Nothing has changed that. Do you understand?"

Her breathing quieted and she gave a curt nod of her head.

Slowly I withdrew the hand from her mouth and as she remained quiescent, I released a tense sigh. I helped her to her feet. "Now, you must listen to me, Caroline," I pleaded urgently, desperately wishing I could read the expression in her eyes. "Essentially we desire the same goal: to stop your uncle trafficking in foreign agents. Is that not so?"

"Yes, of course. You know that to be true," came her tight, breathless answer from the dark.

"Last night, Caroline," I reminded her grimly, "when you confronted your uncle, you intimated that should he not cease his activities, some power lay within your hands to force his compliance. You must tell me the nature of the evidence you hold against him. It's imperative."

She moved restively under my touch, and I sympathized with her inner torment. Pulled between conflicting loyalties, what doubts and what anguish must have coursed through her mind at that moment. I prayed that our relationship so newly forged these past hours could withstand this crucial test.

Close by, Cedric shifted his weight uneasily as he stood in the wet grass. In the labored silence, the horses sighed and snuffled, eager to be housed again in warm, familiar surroundings.

Those brief seconds measured a year as Caroline deliberated, my heart plunging a thousand times.

"Damn you, Pettigrew," she raged quietly through clenched teeth. "You ask too much! What am I to do? Deliver into your hands the axe by which the queen may lop off my uncle's head? For all the days of my recollection it has been he who housed and cared for me. It is he who—"

"And am I to believe that he received you, a poor starving waif on his doorstep," I interjected archly, "without a farthing to console you?"

"Nay," she defended stoutly. "An orphan mayhap, poor in loving relations, but an heiress just the same."

"Ah, I see. Then he consoled your loneliness and your fortune as well."

Her breath came in an angry rush. "Pettigrew, you—you devil! I would—"

"Enough, madam!" I commanded coldly. "No matter one's point of reference, the truth remains the same. He is a traitor who plots the death of Elizabeth! Can you condone his actions?"

"Devil!" she spat. "You know that I do not! I—" Words choked her and I hated myself for my harshness.

Roughly I pulled her into my arms, my lips against the soft hair. "Oh, Caroline, my dear one, let us not tear at one another like this," I pleaded. "I don't want to hurt you, but there's a task here that must be done. I can achieve it only with your help."

My beloved sighed against me, her cheek pressed tightly against my chest, her arms a vise around my waist. Caroline's slender frame shuddered with the conflict of warring emotions and under my hand her thudding heart leaped like a wild creature thrashing to be free.

When finally she spoke, her voice was flat and lifeless. "There's a small ebony box within my uncle's chambers," she said dully. "It contains a list of persons he has infiltrated and the identities they have assumed. If you gain control of that information you will possess all the evidence you require to destroy him."

I shared my lady's turmoil. I wanted only to assuage her despair. Once I revealed the plot, would it truly matter if Ormsby dangled from a hangman's gallows? At the very least his deeds would cause his exile from his homeland, stripping him of property and titles. If he conspired again, let other zealots bring him to be judged before blind justice. I would have fulfilled my pledge to the queen. Did I not owe some allegiance to the woman I loved and the life we would share together? I lowered my chin to rest lightly on the top of Caroline's head. "I will not allow your uncle's blood to divide us, my dear," I told her. "If I gain this information, he will be free to go. . . ."

A stunned silence followed my declaration, as surprising to my ears as to Caroline's. She pulled back slightly, peering up into my face. "You mean it, Pettigrew? You would allow him to leave this place unshackled?"

"We are all robbed of choice, my lady. If we are to live in any semblance of peace, there must be concessions on the part of each."

"But how? How can you justify such an action to the queen?" she pressed.

"Ah, my lady, you race ahead of me in this affair of connivance. I have just invented the game. Pray give me time to contrive the rules."

My Caroline weighed my meaning and apparently found it valid. "Yes, you are right, Pettigrew. Let us be done with this macabre game that wagers lives and fortunes."

With our mission entrenched in our minds we rode directly toward the gates of Tregenna, Cedric trotting at our heels. Once inside we wasted no time dismounting and returning the horses to the custody of the burly stableman, who eyed us with a hard, unblinking stare. As we entered the main hall, we noticed a servant retreating down the hall to the kitchen. "I think that we are just in time for dinner, my lord," Caroline said, glancing meaningfully toward the dining hall. "My uncle should be taking his sherry before the fire. I should think it an excellent time to gain access to certain rooms above." Her head held high, she glided regally toward the entrance to the dining hall. Pushing the door open she stood framed in the doorway. "Ah, there you are, uncle," she called in a loud voice. "I would have words with you."

Content we knew Ormsby's location, if only for the moment, Cedric and I bounded up the stairs as stealthily as two poachers pursuing a rabbit. At the landing, almost in unison, we sidestepped behind heavy window draperies as he and I simultaneously spied a guard pacing the corridor in front of Ormsby's door.

"Methinks Ormsby's of a suspicious nature," Cedric observed drolly. From behind the curtain he darted a quick look toward the guard and, satisfied our exit would be undetected, we emerged silent as shadows. Cedric, agile for his years, crept furtively along the wall, I in like fashion close behind. Another cluster of draperies concealed a narrow servant's stairwell and we eagerly leaped into its shelter.

"What now, Cedric?" I asked his panting silhouette.

He jerked a thumb downward. "There's a secret door at the foot of the stairs, m'lord. Stay wi' me and I'll dance ye right into 'is lordship's parlor."

I strongly suspected that Cedric enjoyed this expedition far more than his master. Disgruntled but resigned, I followed. At the small landing below, Cedric went to the third panel of wainscotting down from the molding and pressed its upper ridge, grunting with satisfaction as it swung inward. He bent to gain entrance and I struggled to squeeze the breadth of my shoulders through. Once inside, the panel whushed closed unassisted and I felt oddly as though I'd willingly stepped into my own tomb. Cedric, however, appeared unconcerned. The only cheering note in the black, foul-smelling passage was the desultory tune he whistled blithely through the gap in his front teeth.

"What goes, Cedric?" I demanded. "I do not intend to

spend my evening inhaling the noxious stink of this filthy hole! There's no seeing a hand in front of one's face." Reaching out, my fingers touched Cedric's bent head.

"Patience, lad," he counseled mildly. "There be a candle hereabouts somewhere. It were the one I used earlier. . . . Ah, here it is. Must o' rolled down the stairs."

A flint scraped rock, and shortly the single eye of Cedric's taper peered into the darkness. In a maze of stairs and landings, crossing and recrossing, I grew dizzy in the old servant's wake. But his step never faltered and, heartened by his obvious elan, I plunged on. As we arrived at another level accented with the same oak panels as those through which we'd entered, he hushed me to silence and, snuffing the candle, drenched us in darkness.

With only our fingertips to guide us, we fumbled blindly into the dank, musty cavity. I estimated the space to be about eighteen inches in depth, allowing Cedric and me to stand cramped shoulder to shoulder. A narrow seam of light bisected the darkness, still permitting a remarkably clear view of the inner chamber if I craned my neck to the side.

Two men occupied the room. A swarthy gentleman, foppishly dressed in pale blue satin and frothy lace, sat at the desk poring over several documents scattered before him. A youngish fair-haired man sprawled in a chair nearby. The smooth planes of his face and the guileless blue of his eyes somehow tickled my memory, and I suspected that I'd seen or met him previously at Elizabeth's court. He draped himself over the arms of the chair, his long legs extended toward the fire. "Do hurry on, Amyiot," he urged pettishly, addressing the man at the desk. "By this time you should very well have those arrangements committed to memory."

Not bothering to respond, Amyiot waved the other off with a dismissing flick of his hand as he continued to read.

Amyiot! The name clanged a warning bell in my brain, but where had I . . . ? Of course! Last night Ormsby pleaded for Caroline to remain at Tregenna to await Amyiot, the personal agent of the Duke de Guise. And at dinner, he'd made a special point of Caroline's getting me away from the castle today. Apparently he'd not wanted either of us aware that these two men had arrived on a schedule different from the one he'd quoted. Alerted, I strained to hear the conversation, a clawing urgency welling up from the pit of my stomach. There was suddenly too much happening too fast at Castle Tregenna.

Amyiot, his head still bent studiously over his task, waved for the approach of the young man, whom I now recognized as Sir Edward Bennington. I also remembered the latter's fawning, obsequious manner when I'd last seen him in the presence of the queen. At that time I'd observed his elegant dress and the weight of the gold chains around his neck and it occurred to me that his manner and person were somehow incompatible. He had struck me as a character out of place; an actor who mouthed inanities while a sly gleam in his wide blue eyes bespoke a shrewd intelligence. With no reason to question the young courtier's integrity, I had shrugged aside my faint suspicions. Sir Edward disengaged his arms and legs from his chair and, with a pained air, sauntered three steps to lean against the desk and look over the Frenchman's shoulder.

Amyiot tapped a page with his feather pen. "You are certain, Bennington, of the number of guards stationed on the premises of the royal privy garden?" he questioned grimly, not taking his eyes from the sketch in his hand.

Sir Edward grimaced impatiently. "Yes, yes, Amyiot. I've told you a thousand times. Double guards are posted at all entrances. While in residence at Whitehall, the queen meets privately with Lord Burghley each Thursday at eleven o'clock in the private garden. At these times there are four additional guards posted at the dock and patrolling the garden terraces."

Amyiot tapped his forehead thoughtfully with the feathered edge of his pen. *"Ah, bien, très bien,"* he muttered to himself with satisfaction. "The plan and the circumstances suit our needs admirably. When Burghley arrives at the landing for his meeting with Elizabeth, our boat will be close upon his wake, our men dressed as royal guards."

The insouciance dissolved from Sir Edward's beardless young face, and was replaced by an earnest expression of deadly intent. He took over the outline of the plan. "And I, leading them, shall forge up the central garden walk, overcome the guards and slay Burghley and the queen! She should not be alarmed at the sight of her own personal guard." A fanatical fire glowed in the boyish eyes and he licked his lips in anticipation of the murderous deed. "It shall be *my* hand that strikes down that flagrant heretic! *My* eyes that shall read the terror on her face as she looks upon the devil and the gates of hell!"

Beside me Cedric's quickened breathing echoed the leaping thump of my own heart. The queen must be warned!

Amyiot tilted his head back to gaze up languidly at the young Englishman. "I've never doubted your motives, Sir Edward, and least of all your Catholic zeal, but I must insist that you not simplify this scheme nor underestimate the intelligence of the queen. Each step, each movement of this operation must be planned and perfected until we are absolutely positive it cannot fail. I do not fancy my head upon a pike decorating the royal gate." He smiled ruefully. "Nor do I think you would relish castration and days of excruciating torture, dutifully meted out by Elizabeth's faithful executioner." Amyiot returned his gaze significantly to the scattered papers on the desk. "So perhaps now we may redirect our attentions to the tedious but necessary execution of our project. The Duke de Guise does not suffer failure. And should you not succeed, it would be desirable that you manage to be *dead* as well."

Unable to meet the threat in the other man's eyes, Edward looked away uneasily. "We will not fail," he said defensively, in a grating voice. "I've recruited fifteen lords of the land faithful to Church and Pope. God is with us! We cannot fail in His work!"

The Frenchman drew his brows together in a dark line over his eyes. "Ah, well, yes. Nicely said, Sir Edward," he acknowledged, reshuffling his papers. "But nonetheless, pray apply yourself to the details of this plan with the same zeal as you do your religious inclinations and we shall be assured success—and no doubt you will have your reward in heaven as well. Now, my young friend, one more time. How many guards will be posted at the dock as . . . ?"

For what I gauged to be an hour, Cedric and I stood entombed in the tiny hideaway, scarcely able to breathe, let alone move. Finally a light knock sounded at the door and the two men, first extinguishing the candles, cautiously responded to a muffled voice. Amyiot eased the door open and there ensued a whispered conversation from which I garnered only the word "Ormsby." The pair promptly followed the unknown messenger, whom I had been unable to distinguish as male or female. Once the door creaked shut, Cedric and I set our shoulders to the partition directly in front of us. It gave with little resistance, swinging effortlessly into Lord Ormsby's chamber, lighted now only by languorous orange flames on the hearth. As I had surmised, we stepped through a section of a bookcase, and as a precaution I looked for a volume to wedge in the aperture before it shut.

Squatting down on my heels, my eyes flickered over some of the odd titles jammed into the case. The first book I'd tried to pry loose didn't budge, so forcefully had it been jammed into place. Impatiently I pulled one from an upper shelf and placed it in the opening.

"Ah, good lad," Cedric observed over his shoulder as I set it in place. "I'd prefer not havin' to fight my way out o' this room. I have a feelin' we'll be needin' all our strength this night just to see the sun rise on the morrow."

Ormsby's room was about the same size as my own, similarly furnished in a Spartan fashion, with no excess clutter. Two handsome tapestries hanging from the ceiling on either side of the large canopied bed were the only concessions to luxury.

Cedric, on hands and knees, searched under the bed. "Naught to be found here but a dead mouse, an old slipper and a lifetime o' dust, m'lord," he informed me. He shook his head in disgust, running a smudged finger under his nose.

I grunted in reply as I pulled open the top drawer of a large carved cupboard and began methodically to go through the stacked piles of his lordship's silk shirts and hose. On his feet again, Cedric searched the desk where the two conspirators had studied the master plan for Elizabeth's assassination. It gave up nothing, nor, after a few continued minutes of probing, did the window seats. Both

Cedric and I pulled aside the heavy wall hangings and still could find no trace of a hidden compartment or concealed exit. We stripped aside the carpets. Nothing. Across the dimly-lighted room we stared at one another.

Cedric's taut, worried face betrayed the same consternation that weighed inside me like a leaden fist. The old man's mouth drooped, despair mirrored in the wide, blinking eyes. "A small ebony box, the lady said, right, m'lord? Could—could she have lied?" he asked hoarsely, his gaze falling away from mine.

"It's *here*, Cedric," I insisted angrily, not willing to even consider that Caroline could have played me false. "It's *here*, man, I tell you. We've just overlooked it in our haste. Caroline wouldn't . . ." Frantically I attacked the cupboard again, and in silent accord Cedric retraced his own steps in the search. Again, nothing. Frustration gnawing at my nerves, I noisily slammed shut a drawer, too pent up to be reasonable.

Cedric grabbed my arm in warning, his head jerking toward the door. Voices and footsteps approached from down the corridor. Without a word I shoved him toward the bookcase and he stepped through the opening and into the darkness. As I stooped to grab up the tome used for a doorstop, my eyes came again to the lower shelf and the odd titles in a strange patois of combined Greek and Latin. A sudden intuition pinned me to the spot, fear tight and thick in my chest. Snatching out my dagger I forced its edge between the bindings and the side panels holding them in position. Along the top edge my blade met with a resistance that snapped as I levered the metal against it. The false front fell open into my hands. Cedric's frightened face appeared around the corner of the open passage. "Hasten, master, I beg of you. They'll be upon us fer sure. They—" His mouth dropped at the sight of the ebony box.

Fortuitously the box was not locked. My foraging fingers quickly found the information I sought, under some small vials that resembled opiate containers I'd seen in an apothecary in Venice. Replacing the box in its secret sepulcher and shoving the facade into place, I bolted after Cedric. Without a breath to spare I pulled closed the bookshelves on the hidden cubicle just as the hall door opened, admitting Ormsby and his two fellow conspirators.

Again sealed in the dark recess, we had not the leisure to spy further. I pressed the list into Cedric's damp palm. "Take this and the white queen's piece from the chess set and escape from Tregenna," I instructed in a tight whisper. "Use the secret passages you've discovered and flee with all haste. Steal a horse and ride as though the devil himself rode at your heels—for at your heels he may well be."

He started to object in concern for my safety, but I silenced him. "Go for the sake of Elizabeth, my old friend, and do not fear for me. The queen must be saved, no matter what the cost." I heard his tight, convulsive swallow and the ragged edge of his breath choke on a long sigh. His hand tightened on my arm in a hard grip of farewell and then I felt the cool, stale draft from the outside passage against my cheek. In a few minutes I followed.

Chapter 15

It seemed an eternity before I reached my own chamber. Closing the door behind me, I leaned my back against it, allowing the hours of nervous fatigue to engulf me. The dreary stink of the passages saturated my person, reeking in my hair and clothes, coating my mouth and throat. A decanter of wine caught the sweep of my glance and I made for it eagerly, pouring a generous amount in the goblet and downing the fruity vintage in a long, greedy gulp. The wine warmed a soothing path down my gullet, washing away the dust lodged in my throat. Too weary to think, I tottered to the bed and collapsed. But my dreams gave me no respite. I lay in a pit, my limbs spread-eagled to the four corners, a tremendous rock balanced upon my chest, crushing the breath from my lungs. My mouth opened to scream but the cry was sucked from my lips and flung into the maelstrom of darkness that drew me spiraling down into its vortex. Jolted awake, I felt my heart throbbing as if to burst in my chest. The nightmare departed with consciousness, but the weight did not. In the darkness my nostrils filled with the sweet scent of Caroline and I raised my hand to caress her head as it rested upon my chest.

"Ah, you stir at last, my Lord Pettigrew," she murmured drowsily. "It seems I've waited forever to gain your attention." She sighed contentedly and, unbuttoning four buttons of my doublet, ran her hand inside against my flesh. I shuddered at her touch and realized with some humor that in my confusion I had left my shirt at the mill. Warm memories of the afternoon with Caroline flooded over me. Oh, my dear Caroline! What witch's charm have you woven upon my head! I gathered her close against me, her silky head tucked under my chin.

"Did—did you find it? The ebony box?"

"Aye, my love, I found it and more than either of us bargained on discovering."

"And the list? You have it as well?" she persisted.

"Aye, love, I found the list."

The golden head moved slightly, listening, waiting for more. "What did you mean, you found more than that for which you bargained?"

I dropped my hand to the curve of her neck. "Caroline—do you trust me?"

"Trust you? . . ." she echoed, her confusion evident. "Surely this afternoon I proved my love and trust?" She pushed herself away from me to look down into my face. Her troubled eyes had grown wide and dark and I could see myself mirrored in their depths. "Damn it, Pettigrew!" she muttered softly, anger edging her words. "What has transpired since this afternoon that requires my unadulterated trust? Say it, man; do not pussyfoot about the matter! Spit it out! I shall not swoon!"

"Very well, Lady. You shall know the truth as I heard it mere minutes ago from the lips of Count Amyiot and Sir Edward Bennington."

A frown deepened between her brows. "What? Amyiot and Sir Edward . . . But my uncle said last night they were not to arrive until next week."

"He lied, and went to practiced lengths to see that neither of us was present today when they arrived. Don't you see? He begged your tolerance for an additional week because he thought by then your threat to expose him would no longer bear teeth. With Elizabeth dead, who would punish him?"

Caroline drew a long breath. "Tell me the entire story, Pettigrew," she pressed.

I did so.

"So, your servant, Cedric, is now on his way to the queen to divulge this plot?"

"Aye, my lady."

"You promised that my uncle would go free—"

"And you still demand this when you know that he is

not only a traitor, but a traitor motivated by greed and not religious conviction?"

"I know only that he is my flesh and kin and that my conscience would not allow his death to rest easily upon my soul."

"What would you have me do, my Caroline?"

Her hand came up to rest upon my cheek. "I must warn him," she said. "He may still escape to France or Spain, mayhap."

"Aye, to plot again."

She laid her head again upon my chest, her arm grasped tightly about my waist. "So be it, my lord. What you say is true, I am certain. Nevertheless, I cannot be the instrument of his destruction. Too many kindnesses have passed between us."

"He has but used you—you and your fortune. Can you not accept that?"

"No matter, my lord. I must do as my heart dictates."

I never loved you more than at that moment, my Caroline. Proudly foolish. Stubbornly loyal. I would not have changed you for the weight of the world in gold. "Very well, my dear, but accept the fact that your gesture may be a hollow one. He has but to seek out the ebony box to realize that the information is missing and that only you could have divulged its location, if it was not you who stole it."

"My uncle will not harm me," she declared adamantly.

"Sweet, stubborn Caroline—we may bear witness against him. In Elizabeth's courts, our testimony could hang him."

She set her lips firmly together. "Not mine . . . not mine . . ."

"Nor mine, lady. But will his guilt accept our benevolence? I think not."

Caroline pushed herself away from me to sit upon the edge of the bed, her arms wrapped protectively around her body. "Damn you, Pettigrew," she ground out through clenched teeth. "You set my soul in a vise, do you hear?"

I placed my hand lightly upon the small of her back. "No, my dear, the vise is of your own making. Your hand alone turns the screws. But I cannot condemn you for it—only love you."

Holding back her tears, she turned her head so the fine line of her profile was outlined by the candlelight. "It would have been better had you gone with your man from this place."

"And left you behind to an uncertain fate?" I asked. "Surely in your heart you know that I could not do such a thing. Would it be too much to ask the same charity you lavish so abundantly upon your uncle?"

She grew still, the curve of her cheek still turned to me. "And again I must ask your indulgence," she said hesitantly.

"What is it, Caroline? Let there be no riddles between us. Say your meaning."

"I—I fear for your life, my Pettigrew. By telling you of that damnable list I placed not only your life in jeopardy but also the life of someone else I hold dear."

I raised myself up on my elbows, jealousy clawing at my breast. "If you speak of André, Caroline, then indeed you endanger his life by merely mentioning his name to me." I spoke coldly although a raging heat seemed to burn inside me. "What is this man to you, Caroline? Speak! I demand to know!" Angrily I flung myself off the bed and strode around to confront her.

The face she raised to me was drawn and drained of all color. She tossed back the bright hair, her eyes narrowing, angry tears brimming upon her lashes like points of fire through golden wine. "You demand too much, my lord," she stormed. "Who are you to charge into this place and set us all on our ears?"

"He has asked you a question, Caroline. Will you not tell him and ease his anguish?"

In the heat of our words, neither Caroline nor I had heard the door open. Now she and I, both startled, whirled to face the speaker.

André stood calmly with his back to the closed door. An amused smile curved the well-shaped mouth.

"Well, my dear?" he prodded gently.

My mouth dropped open and I gaped like a fool. The André I knew was a dashing young courtier I'd first spied in the courtyard leading a troop of soldiers; he who'd so proudly swung down from his horse to challenge me with a waist-deep bow and a flourish of his plumed hat. Indeed, the eyes were the same, their gaze direct and lively though perhaps more sober now. He returned my stare calmly as I ogled the priest's black vestments that he wore and the silver cross that hung around his neck. My mind staggered at the significance of what my eyes conveyed.

"I've just come from saying mass at Langfrey," he told an anxious Caroline, who clung to his arm. "Do not fear. All is well, my dear." He smiled in reminiscence. "It was a worthy gathering, little sister. Many traveled great distances from the surrounding villages. Each time I see such a group and read the devotion on their faces and the joy evinced at my mere presence, I am doubly humbled to know that I may serve God in this way."

Caroline turned away, clamping her lips together against rising tears. "Oh, but André, you risk too much. I couldn't bear to lose you when we've just now found one another."

André, for I knew not how else to name him, glanced up and gave me a sly wink. "I looked for you at the service, Lord Pettigrew, but I did not see your face among the faithful. May I still hope to convert you?"

"For the present, Father, my only conversion will be from bachelorhood to the state of wedded plurality."

He gave a short merry laugh, his head tilting back to show strong white teeth. "I note that you did not say wedded bliss, my lord. Caroline has obviously acquainted you with the prickly side of her feminine nature . . . and yet you persist in your suit. I suspected you of bravery, sir. Now I am certain of it." He ducked aside, his grin widening as Caroline feigned a light punch to his ribcage.

Caroline raised her face heavenward. "Is there no escape from such rogues that discuss me over the top of my head as though I were a cow for barter?"

Indeed, over Caroline's head André shook his head in a sort of amused resignation.

I addressed André: "It would seem, sir, that I've wasted the ire of much jealousy upon a man Caroline indeed loves as a brother. Did neither of you bear any compassion for this poor, uncertain heart? In truth, you are her kin? I confess, in my mind your foreign bearing would have confounded such a possibility."

"I thought as much," he replied archly. "And Caroline and I played to that advantage. She was apprehensive lest my identity be discovered and my neck offered up to a rope." His gleaming eyes narrowed. "To answer the other question I suspect dances on your tongue, she and I are in fact half sister and brother. My father, Jefferey Ormsby, married Lisette Furneau in Reims thirty years ago. When she died, I was left to be raised by my grandparents. My father returned to England and later married Caroline's mother." He spread his hands expressively, encompassing a lifetime. "And so you have it."

For a moment the fair, slender girl and the broad-shouldered young priest stood side by side, their eyes focused so intently upon myself that I glimpsed a trace of their filial connection. The resemblance, however, lay not in any physical similarity, but in bearing and in the aura of pride and innate integrity they exuded.

André held out his hand to me and I grasped it firmly. "My instincts tell me that my little sister rests in good hands, Pettigrew," he said. "In the short time I have spent at Tregenna I have become uneasy with the thought of Caroline's future resting in the hands of our uncle. When I arrived I thought of him as a benefactor and savior, but since . . ." He paused, swallowing away some gall lodged in his throat. "I've witnessed such bloody plottings that now the very sight of Ormsby sickens me." André looked down at Caroline, patting her hand, which still lay on his arm. His attention was upon her and yet I knew he spoke to me. "Believe this and know that my only mission here was to bring spiritual solace to fellow Catholics. Never have I schemed to kill Elizabeth nor would I, in malice, kill any of His creatures. I still believe in a loving and merciful God and no edict or proclamation issued by Rome will ever convince me that He sanctions the murder of anyone in His name."

Our conversation came to a startled halt. From the courtyard below, there suddenly burst forth the racket and jangle of riders mounting and setting off from the castle. Raised torches lighted the ominous scene, casting huge leaping shadows upon the walls of the stone enclosure. In seconds a dozen rough-clad horsemen, hooves clattering against the cobblestones, rode through the gates of Tregenna. No laughter or lighthearted banter rose from their lips as they moved with a precision of deadly intent. In the flickering glare, they appeared like haunted riders upon a devil's task, and the sight of them set my heart thumping against my ribs. One thought exploded in my brain. Cedric! They must be pursuing Cedric! Ormsby had discovered the theft of his precious list of spies!

Caroline's small, cold hand crept into mine. "Are—are we discovered, my lord?"

Hastily I drew her back into the chamber. André stood resolutely, hands on hips, legs planted far apart, the bearded chin pugnaciously thrust out. Touched with a mild hysteria, I wanted to laugh at his cocky stance, so incongruous with his somber cleric's robes.

"By all that's holy," he exclaimed, "will someone tell me what transpires in this madhouse?" His keen eyes swept from Caroline to myself.

Caroline looked questioningly toward me and I nodded my approval. Briefly she sketched what we had learned of the assassination plot against Elizabeth and, of course, the incriminating list that Cedric now carried to the queen.

As he listened, the young priest's brow furrowed in speculative concern. Engrossed in Caroline's words, he tapped his lower lip with a nervous thumb as she finished her story. "T'would appear, my friends," he concluded dryly, "that we are all firmly perched upon a lighted powder keg and the fuse's sizzle grows loud in my ear." His eyes met mine in an intense gaze. "I would suggest, my friend Pettigrew, that you gather up my sister and flee from this place with all haste. Once your man is apprehended I have little doubt that he will be made to divulge your complicity in the matter. My uncle has no reason to question my loyalty, although by now he must suspect that his practices are less than tasteful to me. I shall remain—"

"No!" Caroline's protest burst out. "André, you cannot! I will not leave without you! Don't you realize that if you're found by Elizabeth's forces, as a priest, you'll be hanged?" She swung desperately to me for support in her plea, the amber eyes imploring. "Pettigrew! Tell him he must come with us. It's folly for him to stay!"

"She is right, André." I agreed. "But it is you two who will depart. I must stay and deal with Ormsby."

Caroline's head jerked up, her eyes stricken. "You still mean to confront him? You would not allow him to escape for my sake?"

I took her hand and drew her toward me, kissing her lightly on the forehead. "No, my dear, I cannot. I am bound to stay. If your uncle is as you say, then I have nothing to fear. But the word is out now to Elizabeth, God granting that Cedric got through, and her forces will soon converge upon Tregenna. If possible I must be here to receive them and prevent your uncle from any further treachery." I cupped her face in my hands, kissing the trembling lips. A single shining tear balanced on her lashes and spilled down the pale cheek. "Damn it, Pettigrew," she gulped weakly. "How can I leave you?" She half turned her head toward André, who watched us with a rueful smile on his lips. She seemed to consider her brother for a moment, then drew a long breath and sighed decisively. Visibly calmed, she nodded her head. "Very well," she conceded. "I shall lead André to safety and then I shall return." I started to protest but she raised an imperious hand and would not hear me. "Nay, Pettigrew, my beloved, we shall not argue over this matter. But I will not return here. Instead we shall meet at the mill." Her lips curved in a provocative smile. "You do remember the mill, do you not—my Lord Pettigrew?"

"Aye, witch, I remember." How I longed to . . .

"Very well, then. The mill shall be our rendezvous—in two days' time." We embraced quickly and André and I gripped hands tightly in farewell. "God be with you, André," I said with some whimsy. "But then, I suppose that goes without saying."

He returned my grin with a boyish good humor. "Aye, brother. But I'll put in a good word for you just the same."

At the door he glanced cautiously up and down the darkened hall and then, with a swirl of Caroline's dark red skirts, they were gone.

Chapter 16

Silence weighed heavily, promptly and voraciously consuming the camaraderie that seconds ago abounded within the room. I suddenly felt abandoned and confused and I wanted desperately to run after the departing pair, flinging away the burden of responsibility. Had I not achieved what my queen commanded? Had I not uncovered the plot she suspected? Why could I not now be free to pursue my own life with Caroline? Distraught, head down, hands clasped despondently at my back, I paced the intricately worked red and blue carpet. I stopped, my eyes focusing on the muddied toes of my boots. Obviously what I needed was a bath, fresh clothes, and wine to dispel my loneliness.

With renewed spirit I set upon drawers and cupboards, pulling out hose and linen and—and the new red velvet jacket I'd purchased in London to woo my darling Caroline. On a second thought I decided against calling for a tub in order to bathe. I was loath to have to defend myself while naked and covered with soap. A basin and ewer sat on a small chest next to the bed and I made my limited ablutions, but refreshed myself nonetheless. Drying myself, I struggled into the slim-fitting scarlet doublet and clumsily fitted the ruffed collar about my throat. Cedric would have normally performed this service, and my throat went dry thinking of the peril he might be facing at that very moment. *Wine.* I needed wine to drown my harrowing fancies. At the sideboard I tipped up the decanter. Not a drop disturbed the bottom of my goblet. Hell. Hell was to be with an empty bottle and without Caroline.

I had an overpowering desire to smash the useless container into the fireplace when an uncertain knock sounded at the door. It came again, a light tap-tap almost breathless in its execution. By this time Caroline and André surely flew over darkened tracks across silent fields. And Ormsby? No, that rap was not the work of an angry host. Weary of speculating, I pulled open the door. A young maid with a ruffled cap crammed over dark curls stared up at me, apprehension rife in her wide eyes.

"I—I be Jane, sir, Mistress Caroline's personal maid," she informed me, gulping. "Mistress told me to bring ye these, sir." Awkwardly she thrust Perrigrine's covered cage at me, and from the crook of her plump arm, hoisted in my face a full carafe of ruddy red wine. "She noticed ye be wantin' when she be here, sir." The girl bobbed her head in a self-conscious attempt at a curtsy and started to turn away when nearly-forgotten instructions loomed in her memory. She pivoted back on her heel. "Oh, Mistress said to tell ye, sir, the lock on the cage be broken, and that rascally bird opens the door and wanders about, so ye best be keepin' an eye on 'im, sir." She ducked her head again and with a nervous glance upward through stubby lashes, darted away down the dimly-lighted corridor.

Amused, I followed her anxious retreat for a few steps and then closed the door, beaming upon the timely gift. Perrigrine muttered a complacent profanity from his confinement and I, in need of companionship, threw back his cover.

"Ah, good evening, Master Perrigrine," I offered, feeling in a gregarious mood. "It pleases me to see you looking so fit."

The scrawny bird cocked his bald head and peered up at me with one yellow eye. In a disgruntled fashion he hunched his shoulders. "Bloody bastard," he muttered. "Where's my ale? Where's my ale?"

I shook a reproving finger at him. "Tut, tut, Perrigrine," I admonished. "You must give up this drunken, debauched life you've been leading. 'Twill destroy your liver for certain." I chuckled at my own humor, feeling foolish at the same time for conversing with a bad-tempered one-eyed parrot. As I unstopped the bottle of wine, I sent up a silent blessing to Caroline. Pouring myself a full measure, I drank it down in an eager gulp.

Again there was a knock upon my door, but this time it was a fist that pounded, with loud authority. I knew intuitively that Ormsby stood at the threshold and a cold chill snaked against my backbone. Smoothing my beard, I set down the goblet next to Perrigrine's cage and answered Lord Ormsby's knock.

"Ah, good evening, my dear Pettigrew." He greeted me with that affable joviality I found so irritating. "I've played a poor role as host and I mean to make it up to you. May I enter?"

With a bow of my head, I stepped back. Ormsby strode into the room. He had the same swaggering gait I first remembered seeing as he entered the dining room the night before. To my surprise, he was again dressed as though for travel, in a simple leather doublet and dark, sturdy breeches more suitable for a lackey's wear, I thought, than for a lord of the land.

"Pray be seated, sir," I invited, indicating two chairs drawn to the waning fire. "May I offer you some very fine wine your niece has just sent?"

He smilingly declined with a wave of his hand and, settling into the chair, stretched his legs out toward the warmth of the declining flames. I sat in the high-back chair facing him and as I did so, there came into my mind another time—the day in Venice when I'd sat thus, across from the Hassan Aga. That meeting had inaugurated the parade of events that had led to this moment. I wondered if somehow this encounter would end it. I brushed away the thought and concentrated on my host, who regarded me with half-closed eyes. The corners of his mouth still curved but the attitude of benevolence had fled, and he watched me with the veiled intensity of a spider observing a moth's entrapment in his web.

I found myself unable to take my eyes from Ormsby's face and as I stared, his dark features slowly contorted into a gloating mask of evil. I shook my head, trying to blink away the awful vision that blurred and became double. The two-headed monster leaned forward, asking solicitously, "Are you not well, my Lord Pettigrew? Perhaps a little wine."

Dully I looked over at the sideboard. The door of Perrigrine's cage stood open and the clumsy bird was waddling like a drunken sailor toward my cup. He peered curiously into it and lowered his head. I heard him slurping a drink. He dipped his head a second time and then stood still, the yellow eye looking directly at me. Then he uttered a pathetic little whimper and fell over on his back.

A pain like a dagger's thrust tore into my vitals and with a moan I crumpled forward, clutching at the chair's arms so I would not plunge headlong to Ormsby's feet. Fire burned in my throat as I fought to raise my head and accuse my murderer.

"Poison . . . You poisoned me . . ." I gasped my words a tortured whisper.

The blurred apparition feigned the voice of injured innocence. "I, sir? You would accuse me of such a deed? Why, in truth it was your beloved Caroline who tipped the vial into your wine, and not *I*." From his pocket he withdrew a small transparent tube like the ones I'd seen in the ebony box.

I remembered pushing them aside in order to find the list of Ormsby's spies. Searing pain erupted in my chest and furiously I jammed my jaws together so as not to cry out. "No . . . no . . ." I choked out helplessly. breath trapped in my lungs. "Not . . . Caroline . . . not . . ."

Ormsby's dark, fading shadow mocked me, his low, odious laugh curling into my brain, destroying the last vestiges of hope.

"You poor fool." He reviled me contemptuously. "Did you really think that in a day's time you'd beguiled Caroline into a love match? She but used you to prevent your spying eyes from seeing too much. Why do you think you've enjoyed free reign of the castle? Do you think me so stupid that I'd allow you to charge unchecked through *my* domain?" His chortling laugh rasped at my nerves like a blade sawing into my flesh.

Unable to hold my head up any longer, I allowed it to

fall back against the edge of the chair. The pain ebbed and flowed, but a blessed numbness, cold and eternal, crept its way through my limbs. Without Caroline there was no cause to live, I reasoned, a terrible sadness filling my heart. I heard a last shuddering sigh escape from my parched lips and . . . surrendered, content to quit a world where treachery ruled over love and honor.

Chapter 17

CAROLINE

While Lord Hap told his—our story, I'd found myself captivated with wonder, with joy, and finally with horror. Had I been locked in stone there could have been no less concentrated immobility. My thoughts had raced with his, reliving that other time with such a vivid recollection that all the events rhythmically fell into an established order. And often, as he'd described a scene or happening, I'd known and seen what he had *not* touched upon. I'd remembered the brown mole she so hated on my maid Jane's cheek. I'd joyously recalled dancing the lavolta with André and our ringing laughter as he whirled me high in the air to the musician's lively beat. And then, too, there had been Valkyrie's dainty, prancing steps and how once when she'd fallen and strained her right front fetlock, I'd nursed her back to health. I remembered and grieved for the man whom I'd loved and who had died believing it was my hand that had struck him down.

Lord Hap's face was still turned in profile to me, the dark head tilted back, eyes half closed in retrospect. He remained seated on the curved window seat, one leg drawn up, his long, slender fingers clasped around it. The red of his velvet doublet shown vividly against the mottled, rain-blotched windows. He sighed, oppressive musings weighing upon his mood, and lowered the black tip of his beard to the crisp white ruff circling his neck. How desperately I wished to feel that soft raven beard against my cheek; to know that beloved body, hard and vital, against my own. My soul cried for tears to salve the wound, but none came, and it wrenched my heart to know that there never could be such release from my misery—just as my arms would never again hold that dear head against my breast nor my body soar in rapture to the touch of his lips. Memory burned its scar into my spirit and I suffered it like a festering wound that was never to heal.

But *why* this awful punishment? What was my guilt that I could see and hear him whom I loved above all and yet be unable to experience the comfort of his warmth and touch? My misguided loyalty to my uncle? In a state of confusion, almost of derangement, I moved haltingly toward Lord Hap, my Pettigrew. "No, my lord," I claimed hoarsely. "I did not betray you. Could you believe that I was such an unfeeling monster that I could leave your arms and callously dispatch you to perdition? Not so! I beg you to listen. As André and I left you, he, eager to be away, went directly to the stables to see to our mounts. Hurriedly I repaired to my chamber to gather a traveling cloak and a few personal items for the journey. I wanted, also, to consign Perrigrine into your keeping. While in your room I'd noticed your wine jug was empty and I directed Jane to bring wine to slake your thirst. But as I rummaged in the drawers I became aware that someone stood behind me. As I whirled, startled as a wren, I discovered my uncle at the door, watching me, his expression unreadable."

He noticed cannily the flowing gray cape swinging from my shoulders. "It would appear, Caroline, that you are preparing to depart from Tregenna," he observed casually, a faint, sarcastic smile on his lips. "May I assume, then, you were responsible for the list falling into Pettigrew's hands?"

We were beyond subterfuge or lies. "Aye, uncle," I answered. "You presume correctly. I warned you of the danger if you persisted in your crimes against the queen. You left me no alternative." The memory of his deliberate lie rose to taunt me. "And what of last night when you pleaded a week to settle your affairs, when all along you expected Amyiot and Sir Edward this very day?"

He shrugged away the accusation but I detected a suffusion of color rising to the already ruddy cheeks. He lowered his head, looking up at me from under grizzled brows. "All these years, Caroline, you've been child and daughter to me. Does all that time carry no balance against the weight of the crime?"

I fidgeted with the drawstring bag I'd chosen to house my few belongings. "I—I must heed my conscience, Uncle. I—"

He stepped forward, hands on hips. "And does your conscience require my head on a plate, Caroline?"

In frustration, I flung the bag across the room. "In God's name, you know that is not the case, Uncle!" I shouted. "I wanted only that you cease your seditious acts, but not that you pay with your life! Never was that my intention."

He shook his head sadly, mournful eyes fixed upon the carpeted floor. "This Pettigrew has turned you against me, child," he lamented. "I would not have thought it possible that a stranger could enter my house and alienate those closest and dearest to me."

It was at that moment that my vision seemed to clear. I felt oddly dispassionate as I watched my uncle give the performance that hitherto I'd found so convincing. His head sunk low on his chest and his arms hung in listless defeat at his sides. I thought that perhaps I even detected a despondent tear glistening on his flushed cheek. I might have laughed had not his treachery been so complete. But still—he was my flesh. Depressed and weary of his games, I sighed. "Very well, Uncle. I am no match for your histrionics. What would you have me do?"

I should have recognized the evil little pinpricks of light that leaped into his eyes at my question. But I wanted only to be done with this deplorable business, and foolishly I allowed an injudicious loyalty to sway my reason.

Jane's light tap shattered the oppressive tension that gripped the air and immediately her dark head appeared around the edge of the door. She drew back, surprised at the sight of my uncle, but I waved her in. Reluctantly she obeyed, her dark eyes on her master as she entered the room. She edged nervously to my side, the neck of the wine bottle held tightly in her fist.

My uncle's eyebrows raised upward in faint amusement. "And have you taken to drinking alone in your room, Caroline?"

I did not appreciate his ill-couched humor. "Hardly, my lord. The wine is for Lord Pettigrew. He—"

Before I was able to roll the words off my tongue he broke in, ordering Jane out into the corridor.

I turned on him angrily. "What the blazes do you think you are doing, my lord, ordering my servant in such a manner?"

He held up a silencing hand, waiting for Jane to scamper out, and then made certain the door was properly secured. She'd hurriedly slammed the wine down on a side table as she exited and now my uncle strolled to it and, removing the stopper, sniffed the cork. Slowly he raised his eyes to meet mine, a slow, cunning smile curling his lips.

"You asked what I would have you do, my dear? Perhaps there is a solution for all of us."

Like a fool I listened, believing that some innate goodness still lived in that man. His plan was a simple one. He possessed some harmless but potent sedatives. Had they not been observed when ransacking his private papers in the ebony box? he asked slyly. It would be a simple matter to slip the potion into the wine. Pettigrew would not suspect a gift from his lady's hand. As he slept, my uncle, André and I would ride to freedom. By the next day the draught would have run its course and Pettigrew would still be able to meet me at the mill.

I cringe when I think of how he handed me those poisonous vials and I so trustingly poured their contents into the decanter. What a monstrous revenge he exacted for my exposure of him. How could I have not sensed the malice he held in his heart for me and my beloved?

My hand impulsively went out to touch Lord Hap's downcast head. But midway the fingers froze. In spite of our once shared intimacy, an awkward shyness settled over me. "You *do* believe me, do you not, my lord?"

Of course my hand met nothing but vacant air, and

dejectedly I let it fall to my side. "Please say that you believe me," I implored, almost without hope.

He looked up, his gaze sad and pensive beneath the arched brows. "Of course I believe you, my dear Caroline. I needed only to hear it from your own lips to realize the truth of it." He shook his head slowly, lips pressed together in dispirited wonder. "Even though Ormsby's last words damned you, Caroline, and I knew that death stood like a dark wraith at my side, I could not find it in my heart to accept his indictment of you." Absently he pulled at the point of his beard. "Perhaps my vigilance these past years has been merely to bear witness to your innocence."

I was puzzled. "But if that were the situation, wouldn't that information have released you from this—this purgatory?"

He weighed my remark. "Aye, my dear, you have reason there. And obviously there has been no change in our status."

We looked at each other, both speaking at the same time. "Ormsby!"

Of course! He had been our relentless nemesis from the very beginning. He'd plotted and schemed and murdered and escaped unscathed. He *must* be the key to our present dilemma as well. Was it not his unexpected call that brought me scurrying to Tregenna?

Lord Hap abruptly raised a hand for silence.

Approaching down the corridor, Aunt Elvina's voice sang to us. "Halloooo . . . Lord Hap? Caroline? . . . Where *are* you? . . . Hallooooo . . ."

I looked questioningly at Lord Hap. "I was pretty excited a few minutes ago. Do you suppose she picked up on my vibes?"

He shrugged and flowed toward the door, through it and into the hall.

"We're here, dear Lady Elvina," I heard him say. "What matter causes you to seek us when the clock so recently chimed the twelfth hour?"

I could not hear her muffled answer.

She entered the room followed by Lord Hap and glanced swiftly around. She blinked her round, goldfish eyes as though she found it difficult to see. "But—but where is Caroline?" she asked, perturbed. "I wished to speak to both of you. Has something happened to her?" Elvina turned her doleful face to Lord Hap, who merely looked confused.

"Do not concern yourself, dear lady," he assured her, shrugging at me. "Caroline is here and but a few feet away. Can you not see her? She stands by the window and smiles you a greeting."

Elvina thrust her chin forward, turning her head from side to side as though trying to peer through dense fog. She brightened. "Oh, yes, I do see you now, Caroline," she chirped happily. "But how odd—I'm having a great deal of difficulty bringing you into focus, my dear. Your image is blurred." She blinked her great round eyes several times, bringing her brows together in an almost pained effort. "Ahhh. I think I have you now, Caroline," she murmured distractedly.

Always courtly toward the old woman, Lord Hap's voice was now edged with a slight impatience. "What brings you to us, dear lady?"

Without preamble, Elvina thrust a small white card into Hap's startled face. I realized it was a small photograph.

"I just developed it," she said breathlessly. The point of her pink tongue licked at her lower lip and her gaze darted from Lord Hap to myself. "Earlier this evening I tried to show Peter that I could shoot a ghost with infrared film—when there was a terrible disturbance. I knew that it wasn't *you,* my lord, because you're always so mannerly and that just wasn't your style. But then an odd thing happened. Suddenly the camera flew out my hands and fell on the couch, firing as it did so." Elvina paused, considering her words. She pursed her lips in a rosebud pout, and lifting her eyes, fastened them shrewdly on Lord Hap. "May I conclude that you were responsible for that little accident, my lord?"

He did not answer, but the mischievous glint of his smile confirmed her guess. With Lord Hap on one side of Elvina and me on the other, we pored over the small print.

Elvina's brow wrinkled with her absorption. "Binky and I just developed the negative and frankly, I don't know what to make of it. I'd hoped to capture *your* likeness, my Lord Hap, but instead . . ." She tapped the picture with a gnarled, arthritic finger.

Neatly framed were the features of Lord Ormsby, but because of the camera angle, the distortion marred the perspective. The camera had gone off close to the floor, deflected as it bounced off the settee, catching Lord Peter under the chin, sketching the flared nostrils and the gray crescents of his shocked eyes. But most startling, there appeared over his shoulder and hovering just under the crossbeam of the ceiling a *second* image of Ormsby! The exposure captured this second figure in a fit of impotent rage. The mouth was open and appeared to be screaming in silent blasphemy while his arms thrashed excitedly. Wild eyes glared down upon the unknowing company in the salon.

Elvina drew in her breath, cracking nervously. "What—what do you make of it? I see what I see, and yet cannot give a name to it without—without . . ." She gulped and again searched our faces for an answer.

"Could it have been a double exposure?" I ventured.

Elvina shook her head. "No—no, Caroline. I just loaded the infrared film and only one shot was exposed."

Lord Hap studied the snapshot thoughtfully. "If it is as you say, Lady Elvina, and the film may record the images of ghosts—and Lord Ormsby appears in human form and as a *reflection* of himself, may I submit the possibility that, uh, that some, uh, mishap may have befallen your brother and that indeed, he may be a . . ." Lord Hap bit back on his intended meaning, casting me a helpless look of supplication.

Unable to help, I merely shrugged my shoulders.

Elvina finished the sentence for him. "That he may be a ghost—eh, my Lord Hap? That of course, suggests foul play, does it not? And you are both too considerate to inflict pain upon one who is so obviously old and frail as myself." Elvina lifted thin shoulders. "When I first viewed the negative it crossed my mind that Peter was no longer of this earth." The wan smile widened beatifically. "Dear friends, I *cannot* tell you what a marvelous sense of freedom that realization gave me. So let's consider, shocking as it may be, that Peter Ormsby, Lord of Tregenna, is at this time a member of the spirit world. Which brings to mind the question . . ."

Lord Hap and I stared at one another. The Lord Ormsby we'd seen and heard a few hours ago in the salon had to be an impostor!

Elvina nodded with satisfaction. "Exactly!" she exclaimed. "There's an impostor at Tregenna posing as my brother. Although"—she allowed—"the fake Ormsby has certainly been a marked improvement over the old one. When he started to show some gentlemanly consideration for me, for whom he'd displayed only contempt during my entire lifetime, that was a dead giveaway."

"When did you first detect some change in Peter's character, Aunt Elvina?" I queried her.

Elvina tilted her head to one side, laying the fingers of one hand lightly over her mouth as she reflected. "Well . . . perhaps it started a little over a year ago. Jason invited a young actor friend of his for a brief stay that extended for several months. He was a fine, sensitive young man who was always courteous and attentive in my presence. His name is Tod Gallsworthy and he's returned on, oh, perhaps six other occasions. I must say, I was always pleased to see him." Elvina's wispy gray brows raised in speculation. "And as I recall, in each case Peter was scheduled to make a trip to London or Paris or some other place."

"Of course," I reasoned. "Jason would want Lord Peter out of the way. They couldn't afford to have *two* Lord Peters showing up at the same time! But weren't you suspicious, Elvina? Surely if there were character changes in your brother you would have noticed?"

Elvina chuckled good-naturedly. "Oh, my dears, you only say that because you don't know what a hateful old tyrant Peter really was. I've lived all my life with his treachery and deceit. If I could enjoy some respite from his ill temper and cruel behavior, why should I question my good fortune? After all, Peter claimed I was mad but he'd never accused me of being a fool!"

It seemed we were all Lord Ormsby's victims.

"Elvina," I appealed. "This morning—uh, no, yesterday morning, Lord Peter called me in London, asking that I come here and make a bid on the Medici set. Did you know of that or hear of anything pertaining to the set that might cast some light on its significance? Why would he offer it to me when there was already a buyer—uh, a Davis, coming this very day?"

Elvina's round eyes darkened in faraway contemplation. "Well, my dear, I'm surprised Peter would have done such a thing, but I *was* aware of Mr. Davis's coming. My brother's obsession with the Medici set almost bordered on the fanatic. It's one of the oldest of the Ormsby treasures. He'd never sell unless the circumstances were extreme."

When I cast Lord Hap a quick side glance, he'd already read my thoughts and nodded silently.

"Perhaps we should take another look at the Medici set," I suggested.

In a few short minutes we regained the library and Elvina disengaged the burglar alarm. She opened the case and held up the perfectly shaped ivory queen for our inspection. Lord Hap frowned at the small work of art, gnawing at his lower lip, long fingers worrying the tip of his beard with the intensity of his study.

He grunted softly. "Of course, ladies, it comes as no surprise that this piece is not from the original set."

I stared at his complacent face until the truth registered. "Of course! The original queen was dispatched by Cedric to Elizabeth! It's unlikely that it would have found its way back to Tregenna. Especially after Lord Ormsby was exposed as a traitor. No doubt, following generations replaced the missing piece with a copy."

A bewildered Elvina returned the white queen to its place and held up the black counterpart. Again Lord Hap bent his dark head to examine the small ivory figure. After a long, silent moment, a flame of discovery leapt into his eyes.

"What is it?" I demanded impatiently. "What have you found?"

He would not answer me but said to Elvina: "Lady Elvina, when the Italian craftsman who carved these pieces made them, he created them with a twofold purpose. He served in a double game: one of intellectual pursuit, the other of intrigue. When Giacomo Gamberti carved the Medici set, the kings and queens were designed with hollow bases, to be screwed into vacant pedestals. Convenient for messages or perhaps a measure of poison, eh, my friends?"

Without prompting Elvina purposefully gripped the black queen in one determined fist and struggled to uncap the base with the other. Nothing happened. Her eyes swept from me to Lord Hap and back to the chess piece. Grabbing up both kings, she determinedly attempted to twist the base from each. Neither revealed a secret compartment.

"Well, well," I offered gloomily, provoked by a new thought. "It would appear that this set is *not* the authentic one you offered to Elizabeth four hundred years ago, Lord Hap, which raises another question."

Lord Hap smiled knowingly and stood back, one fist on his hip. The lively expression on his face told me he too had maneuvered the parts of the puzzle into place.

Unable to subdue her childlike exuberance, Elvina burst out with the answer. "If the Medici set is a fake, what else at Tregenna is less than authentic?"

"Besides the fradulent second version of Lord Ormsby himself," Hap added with a sigh.

I could only shake my head in bewilderment. "I still don't understand why Lord Ormsby found it necessary to run me off a cliff. He already had a buyer—this Davis person from Australia. Why bother to bring me down here merely to complicate the issue?"

Lord Hap lifted one dark brow. "Aren't you forgetting a major ingredient in this jester's imbroglio, Caroline?"

"What do you mean?"

"Need I remind you that we have *two* Ormsbys among our cast of characters? And is it not possible that each took action in regard to the set independent of the other?"

It was my turn to pull at my chin. It was impossible to suppress a twitch of humor as I glimpsed Elvina's expression. She peered wide eyed into my face with the concentration of a fox at a rabbit hole. Enjoying the scene, I folded my arms and tilted my head back. "Well, my lord," I said, "accepting that premise, my guess would be that it was the *real* Lord Ormsby who called me yesterday." I mulled over the facts before continuing. "Let's say that last year I examined the real set and during the course of the past eight months, the original was replaced with a copy. When *my* Ormsby decides to sell it, the news throws his double into a tizzy. The real Ormsby lived in a veritable museum of valuable antiquities and it probably never crossed his mind to check the validity of what he was offering. The fake Ormsby, on the other hand, had already negotiated with the Australian for the sale of the real one and was terrified of exposure and the loss of a big sale. So what does he do?" I tapped my forehead slowly with my finger. "He decides to get rid of *me*."

Elvina was beginning to fidget as I outlined my pat little theory. I could tell by the straight line of her lips that she was humoring me as she said reassuringly, "Well, that's all very nice, dear, and probably quite true. But what happened to my brother? He seems to be the key to this whole situation and as evidenced by the infrared picture, he appears to be dead."

Elvina was right. Lord Ormsby was, as he'd always been, the focal point for everything that happened at Tregenna. Obviously we had more sleuthing to do before all the questions were answered. Crestfallen, I turned to Lord Hap.

"Easy, my Caroline," he consoled gently. "There is still work to be done. Arouse your spirits and we shall be one with the game." His expression softened on seeing my despair, and wrapped in his concern, I rallied.

Chapter 18

For a heartbeat of time, I thought I felt the soft touch of that raven beard against my cheek and the strong, rhythmic pounding of his heart beneath my hand. I stared up into the angular, shadowy planes of his beloved face and saw the eyes grow concerned and his lips form my name, but suddenly I could not hear his words as he and Elvina acted out a strange pantomine. I knew they called my name but I could not hear them speak. The room began to recede into darkness and then crazily advanced again, lighted with such intensity that I raised a hand to shield my eyes from the unearthly glare. I tried to cry out but swirling mists closed in, smothering all sound.

I heard my own voice crying for Pettigrew, my Pettigrew. His name echoed in my ears until I thought my brain would shatter and then in an instant all was silent. As I tried to blink away my terror, the spinning room slowed to a reasonable standstill and again Lord Hap and Elvina appeared to me, their faces drawn and frightened. Their eyes searched mine for some explanation, some reason for this passing aberration.

"Caroline? Caroline!" Lord Hap's anguished voice reached my ears and I flinched at the pain I read on his worried face.

Elvina too cried my name as she looked frantically to Lord Hap for some explanation.

"What's wrong with Caroline?" she exclaimed, almost in tears. "She's fading away; I—I can't see her. . . . Oh, dear, I can't find her anywhere. Caroline, where are you?"

Foaming waves crashed at the edge of my consciousness, their biting cold spreading through me. I shuddered as a searing pain sliced across my forehead. Again the shrill scream echoed, reverberating down corridors that drew me plummeting into a velvety oblivion.

"Caroline!" Lord Hap's voice commanded my presence and slowly, breathlessly, I felt myself drawn back to him. I opened my eyes.

"Oh, my dear," he said in a tortured half whisper. "I thought I'd lost you." His hands went out to me in a compulsive gesture of need, but accepting its futility, he dropped them to his side.

"What—what happened?" I gulped unsteadily, looking from Elvina's white face to the tight, pale features of my lord. "I felt so strange—I can't explain it." I shook my head slightly, trying to clear away the vague blur of chaotic images.

Without warning Elvina snapped out Lord Hap's name and waved a bony finger in his startled face. "She's not dead!" Elvina accused him. "She's not dead and you left her in that wreck to die!"

Hap stared at the tip of the accusing finger. "Not dead?" he repeated uncertainly, horror dawning on his face. He swung sharply toward me. "Oh, Caroline, as God is my witness, I would not deliberately contrive to do you harm! Not if I moldered in this hell hole for another four hundred years! No! Not even if it were four thousand! Elvina, I told you I found her pale and crushed amidst the tangled ruins of that metal contraption. I could not believe that my Caroline had come back to me. . . ."

The room swirled around me. Too many questions bombarded my brain to make any sense. *Could* he have saved me? If he'd acted at once and somehow communicated with Elvina, might I be more substantial now than a mere wisp of smoke? What was I to believe? For an eternity he'd condemned me as his betrayer. And suddenly he'd found that same person totally within his power. How easily the torment of all those lonely, hopeless years could have corroded his reason and made him care for nothing but vengeance. The panic mounting inside of me gave way to mindless terror. I must get back to the car! Perhaps there was still a chance! "Elvina!" I screamed. "Call the police! Tell them there's been an accident! Oh, please, hurry! There can't be much more time for me!"

Elvina's mirror-like eyes threatened to pop from her gray head. "Oh, dear, yes! Call the police!" she repeated in a distracted monotone. "I must call the police. . . ."

I followed her exit anxiously. *Oh, God! Let her be in time!*

She shambled across the library like a sleepwalker, muttering the same words over and over again: "Oh, yes, call the police. I must tell Binky and call the police about poor Caroline. Oh, dear." The door closed on her litany of confusion.

I could not bring myself to look at Lord Hap. I felt his hurt and angry eyes focused on me but I could not meet them. My rational mind condemned him, but my woman's instinct could find no guilt in his action.

As he'd read my thoughts, he'd grown withdrawn, erecting an impersonal barrier between us. "I shall return you to the beach, my lady," he said at length.

He moved toward the door, the proud head high, the tall body straight, gloved in the red velvet doublet. He stared directly ahead, rigidly unseeing.

Why must we always be saying goodby, my conscience shrieked! If I leave him now, will I condemn him to an infinite hell on earth? The pounding surf whispered in my memory; death's cold hand lay upon my breast. If I abandoned him now, would I ever be able to forgive myself? The eternal cycle repeated itself. Once before I'd complacently fled from him and he'd died condemning me. And yet I knew that if I were to save myself, I must return now to the mangled wreck at the edge of the waves.

His back to me, he continued toward the door. "Come, lady," he urged wearily, in a quiet, flat voice. "We must be gone. The storm has ceased its turmoil and the sun peers over the edge of the land to measure the chaos."

Helplessly I trailed in pursuit, taxed with the indecision that tore me apart.

We streamed along the gray corridor. A narrow window at the end of the gallery emitted a faint early morning light, and against it I could see Lord Hap's strong, regular features in profile: the straight, patrician nose and pointed beard above the white blur of the ruffled collar. Once beyond Tregenna, I'd never see that proud, arrogant face again. And if I should be found and miraculously returned to life, what then? It seemed I'd lived more vividly, more profoundly, in the past few hours than in all the twenty-six years prior to this moment. Oh, God! If I could only touch him just before I left! Just to feel those arms around me, to feel the hard pressure of his mouth on mine!

In oppressive silence he and I descended the grand staircase to the central hall. The winds that had dispatched the storm still pressed, and like savage dogs, flung their force against the ancient oak door. Lesser curs crawled beneath it, sending icy trills of cold air scudding across the stone floor. A lone candle, nearly spent, guttered in a blackened wall sconce, awaiting a final hand.

But my ears tingled from another sound. Laced with the clamoring winds and their restless rattle came angry, low-pitched voices from behind the double doors of the reception room. Lord Hap hesitated, listening to the verbal clash of wills. I sensed his curiosity but he brushed it aside and turned resolutely as if to continue to the beach. More intrigued than he, I pulled back and cocked my ear to the panel.

"Caroline!" Exasperation rang in his voice.

Rudely I shushed him. "Dammit, Pettigrew," I snapped without thinking. "Can't you see I'm trying to eavesdrop?" I felt his presence at my elbow and, ashamed of my incivility, turned my head slightly and gave him a quick side glance. I forced down the lump of contrition lodged in my throat.

"I—I'm sorry, my lord," I muttered feebly. The expression in his eyes told me he knew. The apology was not for the harsh words.

"I do not condemn you for wishing to live, my Caroline," he said quietly. "And rightly you *should* live, to love a man of flesh and blood."

I closed my eyes, savoring again for a moment our time together at the mill.

"Yes, I know, my dear," he said very close to my ear. "What we had together was precious and enduring and—"

"Oh, stop it, Pettigrew!" I spat out peevishly. "I wish you'd stop being so damned understanding! I—I don't want to be understood! I just want to get on with business and get the hell out of this horror story!" For the first time since I arrived at Tregenna, I was glad I couldn't cry. I knew for certain if I'd possessed the necessary equipment, I'd be blubbering like a baby. Instead, flustered, I sniffed noisily and again pushed my ear to the door. I heard his low chuckle.

"Why don't you go inside?" he suggested in an amused stage whisper. "It will—facilitate—your hearing—immensely. . . ."

I shrugged impatiently as though to shake off an imaginary hand and then, clamping down on the grin that pulled at the corners of my mouth, I passed into the inner salon.

Lord Ormsby or, according to my own theory, his impostor, stood by the mouth of the same high fireplace that had housed the priest hole. He wore a long midnight-blue dressing gown, and the short gray hair circling his balding pate stuck out as though he'd been hastily called from his bed. He agitatedly chewed at his lower lip, his fists jammed into his pockets in tight balls as he dourly regarded the couple on the settee.

Jason, with his glasses lopsidedly hooked over his nose, still wore street clothes. He held Stella in a tight embrace but by the way she struggled to fight him off, I quickly surmised his grip held no affection.

Stella threw back her head, and the dark tendrils of her hair tumbled over the gray flannel of Jason's sleeve. From her long white throat came a cry of terror that made the back of my neck prickle.

"He's here," she shrieked. "Can't you see, you fools? He's all around us. He knows we killed him!" She gasped, choking on her tears.

Jason's hold tightened and Stella's head sagged forward as she sobbed against his shoulder. Jason's pale eyes met Ormsby's, and to my surprise the latter was the first to look away.

Jason exploded impatiently. "For Chrissakes, Tod, do something useful besides wringing your hands and shuffling your feet! Get me a brandy for Stella. You can see I've got my hands full. We've got to quiet her down before she wakes the servants. All this babble about ghosts and dead bodies is going to stir up more questions than I care to deal with right now."

The man addressed as Tod complied without question. Returning with a generous measure of liquor in a snifter, he stood ineffectually holding it out.

Jason glared at him. "Well, dammit, man, help me with her, can't you? Take her arms or legs or *something!* She's like a wild animal!"

As an experiment Jason relaxed his hold, warily gauging the distraught girl's reaction. Apparently too overcome to fight further, Stella slumped slightly forward, her hands crossed limply in her lap and her long black hair trailing across her pallid cheeks.

Tod comforted her in a kindly voice. "There, there, that's a good girl." He offered the glass to her. "Have a bit of brandy, old girl. Do you a world of good. Come along, now. Do as Tod asks, Stella. You know he wouldn't hurt you."

"Oh, so the pair of you are making *me* the heavy in this incredible farce," Jason snapped irritably. "No one was greedier than the pair of you while we were swapping Uncle Peter's antiques with fakes and peddling the real ones. And as I recall, *Tod,"* Jason went on nastily, *"you* considered impersonating Uncle Peter to be the triumph of your acting career, mediocre as it was."

Tod's professional pride piqued, he drew his shoulders back and, lifting his head, looked haughtily down his nose at Jason. "And just *where* would your tawdry little plan have been without *my* performance of Ormsby to authenticate your beastly transactions? Out in left field, that's where, old chap. It was *my* 'mediocre' performance that convinced Sotheby's that they were dealing with the real Lord Ormsby!"

Jason sighed despondently, acknowledging the truth in the statement and his shoulders drooped. His long, narrow fingers lifted to adjust the lenses that the struggle with Stella had tilted askew. "Yes, yes, of course, Tod. We couldn't have done it without you; that goes without saying. We're just overwrought, that's all. Yesterday placed an unexpected strain on all of us." Jason's voice trailed off dispiritedly. "Oh, if only—"

Tod gulped at the brandy he still held. "Let's not start

with that 'if only' business, Jason. It's a little late for that. I can understand that what happened to Lord Ormsby was an accident. He had a foul temper and when he charged at you with that battle ax . . ." Ormsby's impostor shrugged. "What else could you do but defend yourself?" The actor sighed heavily, running a nervous hand around the back of his neck. "But what I can't understand was the necessity of disposing of that antique dealer from London. Surely you could have fobbed her off until we made this last sale to Davis?"

Jason's voice broke, verging on hysteria. "Dammit, Tod! I couldn't take the chance! Uncle Peter's body was already stuffed behind the wall paneling in the library and—and, well . . . all right, let's face it. I lost my head. Is that what you wanted to hear? I panicked. Besides, you know what condition Stella has been in ever since Uncle Peter had his, uh, accident. Did you want her blathering to strangers about what's been going on? Caroline deVries would have spotted the Medici set as a fake in a minute. We'd have had all of Scotland Yard on our necks!"

My head spun at the simple explanation! Of course! That's why Lord Ormsby had called me! He suspected something was wrong and wanted me to verify it. He couldn't afford to contact Sotheby's because the entire Ormsby collection would have become suspect.

Tod finished off the brandy, staring fixedly into the empty glass. "Ummm, I suppose you're right. Damn!" he exclaimed in frustration. "What beastly timing! Just one more day, and we'd have made this last killing and been neatly aboard a plane for Rio!"

Tearing loose from Jason's hold, Stella erupted off the settee."Last killing!" she screamed. "It's just the beginning, do you hear? He's going to destroy all of us! Let me out of here! I've got to get away from this damn place!"

Both Jason and Tod leaped to restrain the wild-eyed girl whose frail body, clad only in a sheer pink nightdress, writhed and fought against their clutching hands. Jason's fist came up sharply and laid a neat blow just under the right side of her jaw. Her head snapped back and he caught her limp body as she fell, dumping her unceremoniously on the settee.

Tod was horrified. "Did you have to hit her so viciously, for God's sake? You could have killed her!" The gray brows flicked upward in speculation. "Or was that what you intended? Just another accident to number among the others, eh, Jason? Remove all the obstacles and the pot grows fatter for the one who's left. . . . When's it going to be *my* turn?"

"Oh, for God's sake, Tod! Are you out of your mind, too?" Jason spun angrily away to stand facing the dark cavern of the fireplace. His hands knotted behind his back, the sloping shoulders were held rigid. The long, narrow face turned slightly in profile and I saw the muscles bunch and work along his jaw.

Stella's pain-filled moan rose from the couch and Tod went down on his knees beside her. "Take it easy, old girl," he consoled gently. "Everything's going to work out. You'll see, my dear. Things are a bit rocky just now, but it's always darkest just before the dawn. Tod'll take care of you, Stella. Haven't I always said I'd make things right for you? Eh, haven't I?" Clumsily he buttoned the pale pink peignoir, attempting to fold the diaphanous material more closely over her nakedness.

The woman's eyes fluttered open and as she focused on Tod, her arms flew around his neck, drawing him to her. "Oh, Tod, Tod," she whimpered. "I can't stand much more of this. We've got to get away from this evil place. Oh, please, take me away—now!" She raised herself up slightly, laying her cheek against his. "Oh, please, my darling, just take me away and we can be married as soon as you wish."

Jason wheeled from the fireplace, his face contorted. "This scene is all very touching, you two, but running away at this time isn't all that easy. There's only a few more hours before Davis arrives. We've got to stick it out until then. There's three million dollars at stake and I'm not going to allow your maudlin sentimentality to interfere with the completion of this sale!"

Suddenly everyone at the scene froze in place. Tod still held Stella in his arms. Jason stood over them, a startled figure balanced awkwardly on one foot, his head turned expectantly toward the windows overlooking the courtyard. In the distance trilled the monotonous howl of a police siren, swelling as it drew nearer and nearer.

Stella's piercing cry split the silence as her legs jack-knifed upward, thrusting Tod roughly aside. "I'm getting out of here," she gasped. Arms outstretched, she stumbled forward toward the door as a cold rush of air spun through the room with the force of a cyclone. Its impact slammed Stella against the wood paneling, where she stood terrified, impaled upon the smooth surface by the spinning thrust of the whirlwind that plastered her hair and gown to the oak boards. A high-pitched scream tore from her throat, slicing through the tense atmosphere like a knife through flesh. "He's here," she sobbed frantically. "Oh, God, he's here!"

Lord Hap and I looked at one another. His perplexity mirrored my own. He and I were both convinced that the sinister presence whipping about the salon was Lord Ormsby arbitrarily revisiting his murderers. But why couldn't *we* see him?

The crystals in the chandelier overhead clinked daintily in the wake of the rampaging spirit. I glanced up to find Perrigrine clutching at a looped strand of glass beads like a drunken acrobat. He swayed complacently and, observing my interest, bestowed on me a pronounced, familiar wink. Insufferable bird!

Again stirred to fury, the ghost of Ormsby flung the full force of his anger against the two men and the terrified Stella. The heavy velvet drapes stood out from their metal rods, caught in the forceful grip of the surging tempest. Mirrors and pictures trembled and rattled on the walls, the metal wires so weakened on some that they crashed to the floor in a shower of splintering fragments. Chairs and tables danced crazily over the thick carpets, toppling clumsily to lie on their backs like slain animals. I heard Perrigrine's frightened squawk as he fled his perch, and looking up, I was shocked to see wide cracks crawling across the scrolled ceiling. The huge chandelier quaked in a palsy of roaring sound and then the roof split open and the light fixture crashed downward in an explosion of shattering glass.

Tod and Jason leaped out of the path of the falling fixture. White faced, the two men raced for the door, one on either side of the half-fainting Stella. The trio sped into the outer hall and then into the fresh early-morning air.

Immediately the room fell quiet. Over the ruined salon an eerie calm descended much like the kind one would imagine hangs over a battlefield in the aftermath of war.

I expelled a long, anxious breath.

Lord Hap regarded the chaos and swore philosophically. "Well, my Lady Caroline, Lord Ormsby remains true to form in life or death, managing to sow destruction wherever he goes." He lifted his head, listening. All animation seemed to leave his face and he turned toward me, features phlegmatically composed. "Come, lady," he invited calmly. "The story runs its course. We, above all others, must witness the final curtain."

Outside in the courtyard we came upon Elvina, her gray hair straggling over her furrowed brow as she blinked worriedly at the approaching police car.

I spoke her name but she did not hear me, and even as I stood at her shoulder waggling my fingers in her face, she offered no recognition of my presence. Instinctively she stepped back as a white Jaguar coupe careened out of a side building that housed the family cars. Speeding past, inches from where we stood gaping, the Jaguar showered upward a spray of muddy water. As I jumped aside I recognized the man, Tod, at the wheel, still in the dress and makeup of Lord Peter Ormsby. Stella was hunched at his shoulder with Jason on the other side. His head twisted to the rear, watching the police car fishtail into the courtyard, barely missing their exit. Tod accelerated and the Jaguar shot forward. The police car ground to a halt and a constable jumped out, shouting after the speeding vehicle, "Lord Ormsby! Lord Ormsby!" Unheeded, the officer gave Elvina a respectful two-fingered salute and, jumping back into the police car, dutifully resumed his pursuit of the glowing red tail-lights disappearing around the dense hedgerow.

With an endearing, almost comical desperation, Elvina waved her arms after the departing policeman. "Oh, hurry, hurry! You must find Caroline in time! You must!"

Dear Elvina. The strain of the past night and her concern for me had grooved deep lines between the innocent eyes. She shivered in the cold morning air, drawing a shabby, outmoded sweater more closely around the thin shoulders.

"Goodby, Elvina," I whispered. "Thank you."

The gray head tilted to one side and I thought I saw a tiny gleam of relief flicker in the great round eyes.

"Goodby, Elvina . . ." I called.

Lord Hap stirred at my side. "Come, Caroline. We must be on our way."

"Dammit, Pettigrew! I—Yes, of course. You're right, as usual. Do—do you think there's still time, my lord?"

"Time, my dear? Why, yes," he said quietly. "We have all the time in the world."

Immediately the scene shifted and we hovered over the beach in its quiet limbo, where the guardian rocks awash in the foaming tide watched over the crumpled yellow Escort. The sun's red disk hung above the gray rim of the sea, burning a molten path across the shining waters. Just as it had been in our first encounter here, the sounds of the sea again subsided into a mere whisper. While all the world seemed to hold its breath, the scream of skidding tires sheared through the calm. My head jerked up just in time to see the white Jaguar, a hundred yards up the beach, sail clear of the cliff's edge. As it nosed into empty space, the centrifugal thrust of its slide catapulted a man's body free from the front seat. Grotesquely it tumbled, arms and legs outflung, and fell like a broken doll on a ledge just six feet below the washed-out road.

The hurtling car, its engine snarling a last roar of defiance, continued to plunge toward the waiting beach. It crashed in a fiery burst, orange flame billowing skyward, a violent pillar against the placid morning sky.

Chapter 19

"Dammit, Pettigrew, I won't go! Pettigrew? Let me stay with you! Please, let me stay with you!"

Hot tears burned against my eyelids and I felt their wet path trickle down my cheeks. From a long way off, a cool, impersonal voice cajoled: "Hush, now, Caroline . . . It's all right . . . Pettigrew is here and he doesn't want you to be upset." A firm, capable hand fingered my pulse and then neatly smoothed the blanket over my chest.

I hid behind my closed eyelids, not ready to expose myself to the outside world of flesh and blood humanity. Feet which I imagined wore sturdy white shoes, rubber-soled their way around the bed. Venetian blinds rattled and light fell in a lattice pattern across my face. The long breath I drew was laden with the smells of disinfectant and shriveled roses too long in stale water. "Pettigrew?" I mumbled tentatively, knowing full well that he was not here. She'd lied to me just to keep me quiet.

Rubber soles hurried to the bed. "Caroline?" A concerned pause. "Miss deVries? Open your eyes, dear," the voice coaxed. "Pettigrew is here and wants to see you."

Defiantly I kept my eyes closed. "That's a lie," I accused. "Pettigrew's gone and I wish I were, too." I turned my head sharply on the pillow and immediately regretted it. Intense pain stabbed through my eyes and zigzagged its way across my forehead. I gasped and my eyes flew open. Rubber soles leaned over the bed.

"There, there, dear," the lean, basically unpretty face said under its nurse's cap. "My, but we *are* glad to see you among the living again, Caroline. You have taken your time coming back to us." I focused on the woman's long, pointed nose with dark hairs growing out of the pinched nostrils, and watched its shiny pink tip move up and down as she spoke. She enunciated carefully. "You're at St. Luke's, in Truro, dear. This is April twenty-third and you've been here fourteen days."

I'd been trussed up here like a mummy for two weeks? Gingerly I tried moving my head again. Heavily swathed in bandages, it felt like a vast, buzzing beehive. The pain stabbed again, but if I moved with more judicious care, was not as severe as before. Remaining motionless I allowed my eyes to sweep the room. "Pettigrew? Nurse, you said Pettigrew was here. Where is he? I want to see him," I demanded contrarily.

Faint color rose on the thin cheeks. "Well, actually he's *not* here, Miss deVries," the woman said uncomfortably. "But I'm certain if he knew of your injury . . ."

The low, ironic laugh gurgled uncontrollably in my throat. The tears welled, too, mingled with the pain. No, Pettigrew wasn't here.

The following three weeks slid by, one gray, listless day merging into the next, recording my life in slow-motion frames like an old movie. I'd returned to the living but my brief sojourn into the marginal nether world left me depressed and disoriented.

Dr. Webster, a crumpled old laundry-bag of a man with a face like Albert Einstein, was kindness personified; and the nurses, including old 'rubber soles,' seemed to have adopted me to be the object of their special patronage. Not until I was ready to be discharged from St. Luke's and transferred to a convalescent facility in Exeter did I learn that the staff considered me something of a celebrity.

Gwen Gilbreth, the thin-faced nurse who'd lured me to consciousness, sqwushed into my room with her familiar flat-footed gait an hour before my release. With a conspiratorial gleam, she spread the local newspaper over my knees. The headline was dated five weeks earlier, the day I'd witnessed the white Jaguar plummet to the Tregenna beach. I'd spent a great deal of time at St. Luke's recalling that scene and remembering that one of the men had been spared in the holocaust. But not poor Stella. She'd had good reason to be afraid. I couldn't shake off the nagging thought that the spirit of Lord Ormsby might well have sought and found his revenge. But with a detached curiosity I still wondered just *who* had walked away from the execution.

Nurse Gilbreth's flat chest rose and fell under her crisp white uniform. "Dr. Webster gave his permission," she said, flicking a bony finger at the paper. "He was reluctant to upset you in your condition but since you're leaving . . ." She shrugged. "I guess he decided it was time." The nurse's hooded eyes watched me with a guarded expression, waiting to gauge my reaction. She couldn't know that I'd witnessed the crash from below. I didn't think the newspaper could offer any surprises.

I was wrong. With an air of assumed nonchalance, I scanned the front page and then cast off the facade of indifference and snatched it up. When I completed the article, the page slipped from my numb fingers. Perhaps after all, in the vast scheme of things balanced between heaven and earth, there *was* a universal justice. I thought I could hear it now, clutching at its belly and roaring over the latest twist of events. The police had *positively* identified the crash victims as Lord Peter Ormsby and his secretary, Stella Regis. The constable on the scene had clearly recognized the disguised Tod as Lord Ormsby at the wheel. The real crux of the article, however, was the disclosure of the implication of Lord Ormsby in the peddling of fraudulent antiques totaling millions of pounds. Ah, and now my name made an appearance, but briefly. It was believed that Caroline deVries, a London antique dealer suspecting the duplicity, had been lured to near-death to prevent her from exposing the wily Ormsby. A news photo showed a grieving Jason, who'd been spared in the crash, proclaiming his shocked innocence. He also announced that upon assumption of the Ormsby title and fortune, he would close Tregenna and take a prolonged excursion abroad.

So Jason would go free. My intuition told me Tregenna housed a new ghost. I wondered if Peter Ormsby's sentence would also continue for four hundred years. Ironically, the one crime of which he'd been innocent had brought about his downfall. And Lord Hap? That same sibilant voice told me he was free at last!

Chapter 20

To satisfy myself, I returned to Tregenna. Before Jason Ormsby left England I obtained permission to visit the castle and was allowed free access. The strong sense of attachment that drew and held me to the place was growing tenuously vague like the reality of a fading dream. My footsteps sounded hollowly down the dark, empty halls, echoing back only the eerie solitude of an ancient house closed and shuttered.

From the old servant, Simon, I learned that Aunt Elvina and her Binky had but this past week been married and were now honeymooning in Paris. In my heart I wished her well. Like all of us, she had lived too long under Peter Ormsby's tyranny.

I retraced my steps to the room where Lord Hap had poured out the pent-up history of that long-ago Caroline and Pettigrew. Shafts of pale yellow sunlight poured through the tall, dust-caked windows, and through a blur of tears I thought I could again see the red-clad figure seated at the window, the pointed beard jutting over the crisp whiteness of the ruff circling his throat, the dark head titled back, lost in dreams of another time.

I blinked away a hot surge of tears. I knew the image existed only in my heart. Lord Hap was gone from Tregenna. The electricity that crackled in the air when he was near, was silent. But then the sadness seemed to drain away and was replaced by a pale glimmer of hope. In the vast, complex scheme of life and death, he and I had twice found and loved each other. I clung to the tiny, vague promise that there would yet be another time and place for us.

The following day I returned to London and to the anxiously waiting Cleo. Countless nights at St. Luke's I'd opened my eyes to find the dear woman, ever vigilant, by my side. Filled with a contented sense of homecoming I fell into her plump outstretched arms. Tears of concern and relief glided a silvery path down her powdered cheeks. "Oh, Caroline, you're home at last—you're home. . . ." she repeated with wondering shakes of her head as though she couldn't quite believe it.

As my stranger's eyes gazed about the flat, it appeared as though I'd merely returned from another normal, routine day at the shop. Nothing in my own cozy room reflected any evidence of the events that had rocked my life since I'd last left this house. My gaze roamed from the dainty antique desk in the corner to the fireplace where the ormolu clock ticked complacently in the peaceful afternoon warmth. Squarely set in front of the hearth was the plump blue couch in its printed chintz cover facing a pair of matching sister chairs. The sun cordially streamed through the sheer curtains, splashing a cheerful pattern of light and shadow over the blue carpet.

With a weary sigh I plopped down on the couch and stared blankly into the crackling fire Cleo had so thoughtfully lit. Depression weighed on my shoulders like an old winter coat. Worst of all, I was beginning to doubt my own rationality. Lord Hap and our excursion into the past had been so real—so vital. But now . . . I blinked, trying to clear away the webs of confusion that cluttered my brain. I couldn't seem to focus my thoughts. I rubbed the scar under the short fringe of hair on my forehead. Had I dreamed it all? Had Lord Hap ever existed outside my traumatized imagination?

A hesitant knock at the door jerked me out of my reverie. Dully I opened it to Aunt Cleo. She clutched a handful of mail and my parakeet Siegfried's covered cage. She wordlessly deposited the bundle of letters in my outstretched hand but I could tell by the nervous twitch of the pink mouth and her discomfited expression that something troubled her.

"What is it, Cleo?" I pressed gently. "Please tell me. I know from the look on your face that *something's* wrong."

Behind the granny glasses her downcast eyes flickered upward and then sideways to the cage suspended from her finger. The corner of her mouth tightened painfully.

"It's Siegfried, dear," she blurted out. "I swear to heaven I took such good care of him, Caroline. Fresh water and special feed and his vitamins . . ." Cleo caught her breath feebly. "But this morning I . . . well, I found him . . . dead in his cage." The woeful eyes blinked. "What a pity on your first day home. I can't tell you, dear, just how sorry . . ."

Doing my best to assure her that I was neither heart-broken nor enraged, I finally managed to close the door on Cleo's effusive apologies. I held the cage at arm's length, eying it despondently. "P.S., your bird died," I said aloud, feeling particularly joyless. I set the cage down on the table and reluctantly removed the cover. To my surprise a very animated Siegfried clung unsteadily to the swaying bar. Raising his green and yellow head he belched loudly and closed one eye in a long prodigious wink.

From downstairs the harsh jangle of the front doorbell jarred its way upward, and after a slight pause I heard Aunt Cleo say: "Caroline deVries? Why, yes, sir; she is at home. Who shall I say is calling? . . ."